THE IRRESISTIBLE FORCE AND
THE IMMOVABLE OBJECT

Olivia adored elegance in fashion. Lord Ramsay called Beau Brummel and his disciples worthless fops.

Dancing was one of Olivia's greatest delights. Lord Ramsay thought it was a wanton waste of energy.

Olivia had a passion for riding to the hounds. Lord Ramsay firmly believed that fox-hunting was an unspeakably barbaric pursuit.

Olivia considered that Lord Ramsay was of use only to make the handsome, hard-riding Lord Roger Malverne jealous. Lord Ramsay could not see that Olivia was of any use at all.

Love between this lady who graced glittering balls and this lord who lost himself in musty books was clearly out of the question.

Perhaps that was why it was so out of control. . . .

(For a list of other Signet Regency Romances by Margaret Summerville, please turn page. . . .)

gotten along, since Jocasta had always resented the presence of another woman in her household. Managing a large establishment that included four young children was not easy for Lady Branford and she thought Olivia complicated matters. Jocasta was jealous of Olivia's beauty and popularity as well as Edward's devotion to her. That the servants seemed to prefer Lady Olivia to their rightful mistress was especially irksome.

Not long after the Earl of Westbrook's departure, Olivia's brother and sister-in-law entered the room. Edward Dunbar, third Marquess of Branford, was tall, blond, and handsome and bore a marked resemblance to his sister. However, their characters were quite dissimilar, Edward being quiet and mild-mannered, whereas Olivia was outgoing and strong-willed.

Lady Branford was a tall, distinguished-looking woman of two-and-thirty. Although judged an attractive woman, Jocasta marred her appearance with the haughty, disagreeable expression she continuously bore. As she entered the drawing room, Lady Branford fixed her eyes upon Olivia. Noting the presence of her sister-in-law's whippet on her new French sofa, Jocasta frowned disapprovingly, but made no remark.

"Well, Livy, by Westbrook's expression and his hasty departure, I can see you would not have him," said Edward, sitting beside his sister on the couch.

"Oh, Edward, you cannot think I would accept poor Harold."

Lady Branford sat down stiffly in a chair across from them. "Indeed, Olivia, I should like to know why you refused him. Many consider him a prize. He is an earl and his family is so well connected. I suppose he is not dashing enough for you."

"That he is not dashing has nothing to do with it, Jocasta," said Olivia, resenting her sister-in-law's words. "Oh, I admit Harold is suitably wellborn, but he is the most awful slow top and a dreadful gamester. Why, everyone still talks about how he lost more than ten thousand pounds at some horrid gambling den.'' She looked over at her brother. ''I daresay you could not afford such a brother-in-law, Edward.''

· The marquess nodded and reached over to pet the dog. ''You are probably right, Livy. Yes, you are well rid of him.''

Jocasta frowned at how quickly her husband took Olivia's part.''You always find excuses for rejecting suitors, Olivia, I fancy you are seeking perfection in a man, and I can tell you that you will not find it.'' She directed a meaningful glance at her husband.

''I do not think a woman should hurry into marriage,'' said Olivia. ''I do not consider my years are so advanced that I am an old maid.''

''Indeed not,'' said Edward.

''I was married at nineteen,'' replied Jocasta ill-humoredly, ''and I know many girls younger than yourself who have children of their own. The Season is virtually over. May I remind you that this is your fourth Season in town?''

Olivia laughed. ''I know that well enough, Jocasta. Four Seasons in town and I have eluded matrimony. Why, I am heartily glad of it! Why would I wish to shackle myself to a man for whom I have not the slightest affection?''

''You talk like a miss not out of the schoolroom,'' said Jocasta. ''It is your duty to marry! Surely among all your beaux there must be one you like well enough.''

''Not well enough to wish to share his bed,'' retorted Olivia.

Jocasta appeared shocked and Edward blushed. ''How can you say such things!'' cried Lady Branford.

Olivia burst into laughter. ''Do not be such a stick, Jocasta. And do quit plaguing me about finding a husband. It is so tiresome.''

Lord Branford appeared rather unnerved by the conversation and his wife's glowering expression. ''Yes, do change the subject," he said. He glanced at the mantel clock. "Good heavens. It is rather late. I told Collingswood I would meet him at the club. I must be off at once." Hardly allowing the ladies to reply, the marquess scurried off.

Once her husband was gone, Lady Branford made it clear that she had no intention of dropping the subject of Olivia's disinclination to marry. "I daresay, Olivia, I have not yet said enough on this matter."

"And what matter is that, Jocasta?" said Olivia with mock innocence.

"Do not vex me," returned her sister-in-law. "You know very well I speak of your stubborn refusal to marry. No girl in the kingdom has had more opportunities. Indeed, the wags are now calling you 'Lady *No*livia.' "

Olivia laughed delightedly. "That is too funny, Jocasta."

"I see nothing amusing about it whatsoever. I don't see why you don't mind being talked about."

"One is always talked about in society. Indeed, one wishes to be talked about, my dear Jocasta."

"Oh, yes, it is so wonderful being considered the town's greatest flirt!"

Olivia smiled. "Why, it is a great accomplishment, considering how much competition one has."

"You are impossible," said Jocasta, shaking her head.

"Truly, Jocasta, I don't mean to vex you. I assure you I shall marry in time."

Lady Branford rejected Olivia's conciliatory tone. "I fancy my little Winifred will wed before you, and she is not yet three."

Olivia regarded her sister-in-law in surprise. "By my faith, Jocasta, you truly are upset with me!"

"And why shouldn't I be? This house has had two mistresses for too long."

"Two mistresses? What do you mean?"

"Do not pretend to be so birdwitted. Ever since your

father died and you joined our household, you have done everything you could to make my life difficult.''

Olivia was genuinely astonished. "I don't know what you are talking about."

"Of course you don't," said Jocasta scornfully. "You have constantly usurped my authority! You have come between my husband and myself and have turned my servants against me. They always come to you for your opinions rather than to me. Even my own children seem to prefer you to me!"

"That is untrue!" cried Olivia.

"It is true. Oh, I have found your presence meddlesome from the first. But as I was certain you would soon marry and be gone, I thought I could tolerate having you about. But now three years have gone by and still you have no intention of quitting this household!"

Olivia sat in stunned silence. Although she had long known that her sister-in-law had little affection for her, Olivia had been unaware of the intensity of Lady Branford's dislike. The revelation of Jocasta's true feelings was not unlike a slap in the face. Somehow Olivia managed to reply calmly. "I really did not know you felt this way. I swear that I never knowingly wished to appropriate your authority and, indeed, I do not think I have done so. However, knowing that you feel this way, I shall endeavor to rid you of my presence as soon as possible." Olivia rose abruptly from the sofa and hurried out of the drawing room. The whippet appeared startled, and after directing a questioning look at Lady Branford, the dog hastened to follow her mistress.

Once inside her bedchamber, a very upset Olivia threw herself on her bed and burst into tears. The whippet jumped up after her and appeared as distraught as her mistress. "Oh, Mayflower," said Olivia, hugging the dog to her, "all this time she has resented me. Indeed, hated me! What a simpleton I have been not to have realized it." Mayflower looked sympathetic and Olivia continued. "What a horrid woman! What absurd things she said! Have you ever heard such rubbish, Mayflower? Why, she thinks I refuse to marry just to spite her.''

After some time of thinking herself dreadfully maligned, Olivia grew calmer and rose from the bed. Taking a handkerchief, she wiped her eyes and then walked over to the window. Staring reflectively out at the fashionable London street, Olivia frowned. Perhaps Jocasta could not be blamed entirely. Of course, her sister-in-law was guilty of great exaggeration, but there may have been some truth in what she said. Certainly Olivia's presence in the household did not make things easier for Jocasta. Olivia had upon occasion given the servants orders without thinking what her sister-in-law would want, and she had to admit that her elder brother was very indulgent toward her. There was no question that Olivia spoiled her niece and nephews, sometimes making it difficult for Jocasta to discipline them as she wished.

No, in fairness, thought Olivia, Jocasta had some reason to wish her out of the Branford household. Turning away from the window, Olivia addressed the whippet, who was now at her feet. ''Well, Mayflower, it appears we are not welcome here. There is nothing to do but find a new home.''

Thus resolved to quit her brother's house, Olivia pondered what she might do next. Her options were rather limited, she decided. She could marry, of course, and, indeed, that was the most logical course of action. There was no dearth of gentlemen among whom she could choose, but as various suitors came to mind, Olivia's thoughts grew gloomier. There was not one gentleman of her acquaintance whom she was in the least eager to marry.

''If only I might have my own household,'' she said aloud, and the more she reflected upon this possibility, the more Olivia liked it. How wonderful it would be to live on one's own and do as one pleased. She would tell Edward that she would not need a large establishment, just a modest dwelling in town. Surely her brother would see the advantage of such an arrangement and agree to it. Buoyed by the idea, Olivia brightened.

Then remembering that she was to accompany her cousin Aubrey and his wife, Sophie, to a party that evening, Olivia was suddenly cheerful. Resolving to talk to them about the matter and feeling much more herself, Olivia called to her whippet and went off to take a brisk walk around the grounds.

2

As they often did, Sir Aubrey Roxbury, Baronet, and his wife, Sophie, arrived rather late to escort Olivia to the party that evening. Due to the lateness of the hour, they did not linger long at the Marquess of Branford's town house. Olivia was glad of this, for she was eager to go out. She sat contentedly inside the Roxburys' stylish closed carriage as it made its way the short distance to their destination.

Sophie Roxbury chattered merrily, allowing Olivia no opportunity to mention the problem with her sister-in-law. Lady Roxbury was a loquacious person whom some considered a bit of a featherhead. Although this term was rather appropriate, Olivia was very fond of Sophie and could easily overlook her faults.

Best of friends, the two young ladies had known each other since girlhood. Olivia had been delighted when Sophie had married her favorite cousin, Aubrey. She spent much time in the company of the Roxburys, who were both fun-loving although a trifle silly.

Lady Roxbury, although eclipsed by Olivia's beauty, was quite attractive. Rather short and fashionably plump, she had a pretty, round face, large brown eyes fringed with dark lashes, and a charming dimpled smile. Her lovely dark tresses, voluptuous figure, and lively disposition made Sophie a favorite in society.

Her husband made no claim to attractiveness. Sir Aubrey was of average height and slight build and his plain freckled countenance was framed with curly hair of a startling shade of red. He was cursed with very prominent front teeth and a disturbingly weak chin that gave his face an unfortunate rabbit expression. Although ill-favored in appearance and rather lacking in wit, the baronet was still a popular fellow. His unfailing good humor and friendliness endeared him to many and his great wealth allowed him to entertain in a lavish style much appreciated in society.

Although both of the Roxburys paid particular attention to fashion, Sir Aubrey often seemed consumed by matters of dress. Dedicated to the pursuit of dandyism, he spent vast sums on coats and breeches. He took the greatest care to be always in fashion, hanging on every word of the great Brummell, although, it appeared, with little understanding of the Beau's pronouncements. Therefore, Sir Aubrey was far more ostentatious in his dress than the elegant king of dandies, causing Brummell more than once to lift a disapproving eyebrow at him.

Olivia was well aware that at times her cousin's attire bordered on the outrageous. That evening, for example, he wore a striped coat of scarlet and cream, a scarlet waistcoat, and white knee breeches and stockings. His extravagantly tied cravat was fixed with a huge ruby pin and his shirt points were so high that he could not turn his head. "I say," exclaimed Sir Aubrey, twisting his body to see out the carriage window, "we are here. 'Pon my honor, I hope this will not be a dead bore."

"Aubrey!" cried his wife. "Of course it will not be a bore. Lady Digby always has the most charming company."

'She does have you ladies," drawled Sir Aubrey. "I daresay the company could scarcely be more charming."

"Such flummery, Aubrey," said Olivia, smiling at the baronet.

Sophie leaned over and placed a fond kiss on her husband's cheek and then the carriage door opened and a liveried servant assisted them from the vehicle. Once inside the magnificent home of Lord and Lady Digby, Olivia and the Roxburys greeted their host and hostess and began to move about among the guests.

After a short time, they were joined by a handsome young man in military dress. Espying this gentleman, Sophie broke into a delighted smile and hurried to embrace him. "Reggie!"

"My dearest sister," said the young man, returning her embrace exuberantly. He then looked at the others. "Aubrey, old man, and the lovely Olivia!"

"How good to see you, Reggie," said Olivia. "I thought your regiment had been called out."

"Not quite yet, but very soon. Fortunately, we'll be a few more days in town and I shall take advantage of them. Thank God you are here. This party was a very dull affair indeed."

Olivia smiled indulgently at Major Reginald Baxter. She had known Sophie's brother since they were all children together, and had a sisterly fondness for him. He was a likable young man, although he had a wild reputation and a fondness for drink and actresses.

"Perhaps I should join your regiment," said Lord Roxbury.

"Aubrey, you will do nothing of the kind," said Sophie with unusual firmness.

"You cannot be serious, cousin," said Olivia.

"Oh, I don't know," replied the baronet, eyeing his brother-in-law enviously, "but I should like to wear a uniform like that. You officers are very lucky, you know."

They all laughed. "Yes, we are," said Major Baxter, winking at Olivia. "There's not a lady who can resist a uniform."

Olivia directed a mischievous glance at him. "At least it appears that few ladies can resist yours, Reggie, from what I have heard."

The major grinned and his sister wagged a finger at him. "I do wish you would settle down, Reggie. You should be married."

"Indeed so," said Sir Aubrey. "Marriage is a wonderful institution."

"Good heavens," cried Major Baxter in mock dismay. "Livy, you must come to my rescue."

"I shall indeed, for I am most impatient with persons telling others they must marry."

Sophie looked over at her friend. "Why, Livy, I hope you are not out of sorts because I told you last week a certain gentleman would be a good match for you."

"Of course not," replied Olivia. "No, I allude to my sister-in-law. Why, just today we had a quarrel because I rejected a suitor"

"You did?" cried Sophie. "Who was it?"

"That does not signify."

"But it does," returned Lady Roxbury. "You must tell us."

"Oh, very well, it was Westbrook."

"Egad!" cried Aubrey. "I detest that fellow. Your sister-in-law could not wish you to marry him."

Olivia nodded. "Jocasta would not care if I married the devil himself if I would just leave her household."

"My poor Olivia, you must be quizzing us," said Sophie. "Lady Branford is not so unreasonable."

"She thinks I am too particular," said Olivia.

"And indeed you are," said Sophie. "I have thrown all manner of eligible gentleman in your path and you have scorned them all."

"But my dear Sophie," said Aubrey, "do not be so hard on Livy. She is right to be particular. After all, you were very particular yourself."

The baronet's remark made them laugh, and then Olivia

continued. "I think Jocasta would be very happy if I married the next man to cross the doorstep."

"What a splendid idea!" cried Reggie. "Why don't you?"

Olivia laughed. "Perhaps I shall. Yes, I resolve to marry the next gentleman who crosses the threshold!"

Sophie looked over at the doorway. "How exciting! Why, your future husband will be entering the room at any moment. Oh, look! Here he comes now!" At that moment a rotund elderly man stepped through the doorway.

"Worse luck!" cried Major Baxter. "That is Mr. Bainbridge and he is married already."

"I should think that good luck," said Olivia with a smile.

"It must be an eligible man," said Sophie, continuing to watch the door. "Yes, the first unattached gentleman will be your husband."

They all turned and once again watched the doorway. "This really is too silly," protested Olivia, but the others ignored her.

"Here he comes!" said Sophie excitedly as a younger gentleman came into the room.

Although a distinctly better prospect than Mr. Bainbridge, the man now appearing would hardly have been singled out as a potential husband for the glamorous Lady Olivia Dunbar. He was perhaps near thirty years of age and was of average height and athletic build. His countenance was dark and unsmiling and he was not particularly handsome. Indeed, there was something unsettling about the man. Perhaps it was his wild black hair or the arrogant way his dark eyes surveyed the room. He was dressed carelessly and appeared indifferent to fashion. After pausing at the doorway, he entered the room, limping slighty as he walked.

"Who is it?" whispered Sophie. "We must find out if he is married."

"Good God!" cried Sir Aubrey suddenly. "I do recognize him. Why, it is Ramsay!"

"You know him, Aubrey?" asked Sophie eagerly. "Is he married?"

"No, I am sure he is not married," returned the baronet.

"Good," said Sophie, smiling over at Olivia. "There is your future husband. He is not precisely dashing, but he does have a wild romantic look about him. I do hope he is rich. Aubrey, you must tell us all you know about him."

Olivia, who had been regarding the stranger with great interest, turned toward her cousin. "Yes, Aubrey, I am so curious about the man I am to marry."

The baronet laughed. "My poor Livy. I fear the fates have dealt you a deuced bad hand. That is Baron Ramsay of Hawkesmuir and a very odd fish indeed. I called upon him last spring when I was in Northumberland. I'm sure I've spoken of him. Why, I've never met a more uncivil fellow. His estate adjoins that new property of mine."

Major Baxter broke into a grin. "You cannot mean the man you told me about, the monk?"

"A monk?" Sophie looked puzzled. "Oh, dear, you certainly cannot marry a monk, Livy."

Olivia laughed. "I should hope not! Aubrey, what is this monk business?"

Her cousin laughed again. "It is really too funny. That is his nickname, Monk Ramsay."

"Oh my," said Sophie, "that does not bode well for a husband. You said you met him in Northumberland? I do vaguely recall your telling me about meeting an unpleasant neighbor."

Aubrey nodded. "That was Ramsay. I was told he is called Monk because he is a recluse, seldom leaving his estate. His residence is a frightful castle, a most horrid gloomy place. I felt obliged to call upon him, since he was my nearest neighbor, but I received a very poor reception when I did so. His enormous dog nearly attacked me and Ramsay didn't appear too eager to call the beast off."

"Oh, yes," said Sophie. "I do remember your telling me about that. This Ramsay sounds simply odious. I daresay it was a mistake buying that property in such an uncivilized place among such people. And to think you wished me to accompany you! I am very glad I did not."

"They were not all so bad and I daresay the hunting will make up for a little incivility. Indeed, one of my neighbors is a fine fellow, Roger Malvern. The Malvern Hunt is famous throughout the kingdom and Malvern has the finest pack of hounds in all of the north."

"Then he must be an admirable man," said Olivia with a smile.

"Oh, yes," replied Aubrey enthusiastically. "And his stables are quite amazing as well as his wine cellar. Yes, I found Malvern a likable chap. It was he who told me all about Ramsay. He quite detests the baron, you know. According to Malvern, Ramsay avoids all society, preferring to spend his time reading books and poking about the ruins of medieval abbeys."

Major Baxter shook his head. "This Monk Ramsay does sound very peculiar."

They all continued to watch the baron, who, looking singularly out of place, made his way across the room. "Well, Livy," said Sophie, "I do not think Lord Ramsay will make you a good husband, although I remember Aubrey saying he was very rich."

The baronet nodded. "He is rich as a nabob. His land holdings in Northumbia are vast."

"That is something," said Sophie skeptically. "Yes, Livy, that is some consolation as you set your cap for him."

"I fear," said the major, "that this fellow is so uncommon strange that even Livy's charm would be insufficient to turn his head."

"Scoundrel!" cried Sophie. "How can you doubt Livy's ability to win any man? She has but to tweak her little finger and this Monk would come running."

"Oh, Sophie," said Olivia, "don't be ridiculous."

"I am not at all ridiculous! I wager you would have him

asking for you before Christmas if you set your mind to it.''

"Then I should wager against you, Sophie," returned her brother with a broad grin.

"Reggie, how could you have so little faith in my cousin?" said Sir Aubrey. "One hundred pounds that Ramsay will offer for Livy before Christmas Day."

"Done!" cried the major, eagerly shaking the baronet's hand.

"Wait just a moment!" said Olivia. "I have no intention of being party to such an absurd wager."

"You see?" said Baxter. "Livy does not think she could win him."

"Livy," said Sophie, "do tell my brother you think nothing of the kind. Oh, but your modesty will not allow you to say so."

"I mean no offense to Livy," said the major with a mischievous look. "There is hardly a man in society who is not smitten with her. Why, I am always throwing myself at her feet, but, alas, she will not have me."

"That only shows Livy's good judgment, Reggie," said Sophie, smiling affectionately at her brother.

"You are too cruel," returned the major. "As cruel as Lady Olivia."

"I pray you quit being so silly, Reginald Baxter," said Olivia. "Indeed, let us cease this nonsensical talk. I don't want to hear anything more about this Monk Ramsay."

"I would think you would wish to hear as much as possible about your future husband," said Aubrey. "Oh, this will be such fun! I shall thoroughly enjoy seeing my brother-in-law lose this wager."

"I shall not lose," said Baxter, "for not every man is susceptible to feminine wiles. And by the look of him, Ramsay will be impervious to Livy's best efforts."

"Livy," cried Sophie, "you cannot suffer such effrontery! You must take up the challenge!"

"Very well, I shall show no mercy to the unfortunate

Monk,'' said Olivia with a smile. "He will soon be desperate to marry me.''

They all laughed again. "That's the spirit, cousin!'' cried Aubrey.

"Indeed,'' said Sophie. "You will win the wager easily. Oh, perhaps it is a trifle wicked to take advantage of the poor man, but what a lark it will be!''

"Then let us haste to meet your quarry,'' said Aubrey. "I shall introduce you.'' The baronet led the others toward Ramsay, who was standing by himself and looking not very pleased to be there. Seeing the party approaching him, the baron appeared surprised. "Ramsay,'' said Aubrey, directing a jovial grin at that gentleman, "what deuced good luck meeting you again.'' When the baron only stared blankly at him, Sir Aubrey continued. "You do remember me, don't you, Ramsay?''

"Indeed, I do not, sir.''

Olivia, amused at the bluntness of the reply, tried to refrain from smiling. Aubrey seemed undaunted. "We did meet only once. It was in April. I called upon you at Hawkesmuir Castle. I am Sir Aubrey Roxbury, the new owner of Fenwyck.''

"Oh, yes,'' said Ramsay with a notable lack of enthusiasm. "I do remember your visit now.''

"I would like to introduce my wife, Lady Roxbury, my cousin Lady Olivia Dunbar, and my brother-in-law, Major Baxter.''

The baron bowed stiffly and seemed completely indifferent at being presented to two of society's loveliest belles. "How do you do?'' he said with seeming reluctance.

"I am so pleased to meet you,'' said Sophie. "My husband has told me all about calling on you in Northumberland. I did not accompany him on that journey, for it is so very far from everything. Why, it is hardly England at all, being so far north. Have you just come to town, Lord Ramsay?''

"I have, ma'am.''

"What a pity that you have missed the Season," said Sophie.

"That was my intention," replied the baron.

"You cannot mean you do not enjoy London society, Lord Ramsay?" said Olivia, directing a dazzling smile at him.

"That is precisely what I mean, ma"am."

Olivia's eyebrows arched with amusement. "Is it London or society that you dislike?"

"Both equally," returned the baron.

"Come, come, sir," said the major affably, "you cannot mean that, not with so many pretty ladies about."

The baron seemed to ignore the remark and made no reply.

"Lord Ramsay," said Sophie, "I am sorry you don't seem to enjoy being in town. Perhaps it is because you have left a young lady back in Northumbria?"

"You are quite mistaken," said the baron, regarding Sophie with some irritation. "I will, however, be glad to return north."

"I do hope, Lord Ramsay," said Olivia, smiling conquettishly, "that you will not be too hasty in quitting London. There are too many young ladies eager to meet a new gentleman."

His dark eyes met hers. "I shall stay in town but a fortnight."

"How cruel, my lord," said Olivia. She was about to say something more, but his unsmiling expression stopped her.

"Well, this time of year a gentleman starts to think about hunting," said Aubrey. "There are some famous hunts in the north, the Malvern the best of them all. After all, that is why I bought Fenwyck. I daresay, Ramsay, I can hardly wait until hunting season."

The baron frowned at this remark and the baronet suddenly remembered having been told that Ramsay did not hunt and, indeed, abhorred hunting. "I do not hunt," said Ramsay coolly.

Aubrey strove to cover his gaffe. "Not hunt, you say? Well, perhaps not everyone enjoys sport."

"I for one," said Sophie, "am glad that there is at least one gentleman in the kingdom who is not mad for hunting."

"Yes, it is quite refreshing," said Olivia. "Many of us ladies find the hunting season such a bore."

"Do not pretend that you do, Livy," said Baxter. He smiled at the baron. "This lady rides like a veritable Amazon and is one of the few females welcome in the hunting field. There is not an obstacle she cannot take."

Noting that Baron Ramsay was regarding her with distinct disapproval, Olivia changed the subject. "Is it business that brings you to town?"

"Yes," he replied, not elaborating. "I do hope you will excuse me. I have not yet greeted our hostess." With these words, he abruptly departed, leaving the others to stare after him.

"I don't think I have ever met such a rude man," said the major. "It seemed it pained him to speak to us."

Olivia nodded. "He was most unpleasant, but it was very bad of you, Reggie, to tell him I liked to hunt."

"I do want to win my wager, my dear," laughed Baxter, "and from the look of it, I shall have no trouble."

"Oh, he only pretended to be indifferent to Livy," said Lady Roxbury. "I am sure he was actually quite taken with her."

Olivia burst into laughter. "Don't you think you're doing it a bit too brown, Sophie?"

"Certainly not. However, if he is going to be in London for only a fortnight, it will be difficult. You will have to work very diligently to win the bet."

"Oh, come," said Olivia, "let us forget this silly wager business. It was just a joke, after all."

"It was not a joke," said Aubrey. "A gentleman never makes a wager in jest."

"That is true," said Baxter. "We are in deadly earnest. Come, my lady, I did not expect you to give up the fight at the first sight of adversity."

"No, she will not!" said Sophie. "I shall not allow it." Lady Roxbury looked thoughtful. "We must plan our strategy."

Olivia shook her head but made no further protest as her friend continued.

3

Having returned very late the previous night, Olivia slept long into the morning. Upon waking, she thought of the party and smiled. The wager about Lord Ramsay had been so amusing, and although Olivia had felt a little guilty at their having made him the butt of their jokes, the baron's uncivil behavior made it impossible for her to feel truly contrite. Olivia smiled again as she remembered how they had watched Ramsay's every move. How disappointed they had been when the baron had left the party early.

Olivia had to admit that Ramsay was very different from the gentlemen she usually met. It was rather diverting although a trifle unsettling to meet a man who did not seem enraptured by her from the first. Of course, Olivia was very much aware that her generous dowry was a great attraction to many of her suitors. If Ramsay was as wealthy as Aubrey indicated, he certainly did not have to be concerned about a lady's fortune.

Olivia frowned. She was always very confident of her ability to attract men, and it was something of a blow to find a man who was obviously uninterested. Yes, it certainly would be a challenge to capture Lord Ramsay's affections, she thought. Olivia's reflections were cut short by her sudden realization of the lateness of the hour, and she knew she must hasten to get dressed and go downstairs.

The prospect of once again facing her sister-in-law, Jocasta, was not a pleasant one. The party and the absurd wager had temporarily pushed her problem with Jocasta from her mind, but now Olivia thought again of her sister-in-law's words and resolved to talk to her brother at once about allowing her to establish her own household.

A slight smile appeared on Olivia's face as she rang for her maid. If her brother refused her, she thought, she could always marry Baron Ramsay.

A short time later, Olivia appeared in the drawing room, where she found Edward sitting in his favorite chair reading a newspaper. "Good morning, Edward. Where is Jocasta?"

He looked up from his newspaper. "She went to the milliner's. I daresay she would have liked you to go with her and you not been such a slugabed."

"I am sure she is much relieved at not having my company," said Olivia, taking a seat near her brother. "You know she has never liked me."

"That is nonsense, Livy," said the marquess. "She is very fond of you."

"Rubbish! There is no need to keep up this charade, Edward. Yesterday after you left, Jocasta and I had a very revealing discussion. She made her feelings perfectly clear to me".

"What do you mean?"

"I mean that Jocasta resents my living here. That is why she is so eager to see me wed. She was quite upset that I refused Westbrook."

"Perhaps she was not in the best of tempers," conceded the marquess.

"It is much more than that." Olivia directed an earnest look at her brother. "I cannot blame Jocasta. We have never got along. I know how difficult it must be, having another woman in the household, especially someone like me, who likes to have things her own way. There are bound to be conflicts."

"I am sure you and Jocasta will soon mend this rift."

"No, Edward, it is not the sort of thing that can be mended easily. I fear the only solution is for me to leave."

"Leave? How could you leave?"

"Oh, Edward, you could allow me to set up my own household. I could find a respectable companion, an older woman to lend countenance to my situation. It would not have to be a large house. Something small in town would do nicely. I promise I would not be extravagant. Don't you see it would be the best thing for me to do? We should all be so much happier. Do say you will allow it."

Her brother regarded her in some surprise and then seemed to consider her words. "It would never do, Livy. You are too young. Perhaps if you were older."

"But I am two-and-twenty. Indeed, Jocasta thinks me an old maid."

Edward shook his head resolutely. "It is out of the question. A young girl cannot live alone."

"But I would not live alone. I know I could find a suitable companion."

"The answer is no," replied the marquess, speaking with uncharacteristic firmness. "You are simply too young. Now, I do not want to hear another word on the subject, Livy. You must patch up your quarrel with Jocasta and that will be the end of the matter."

Olivia's color rose and she got up from the chair. "You are unreasonable, Edward. I can see I should have accepted Westbrook. Perhaps I shall."

"Don't talk like a schoolgirl," said Edward, putting down his paper and frowning.

Before Olivia could reply, the butler entered the room and announced the arrival of callers. "Sir Aubrey and Lady Roxbury, my lord."

Edward frowned again. "I expect we will have to see them," he said. "Very well, Jenson, show them in."

The butler bowed and left them and Olivia shook her head. "I don't know why you don't like Aubrey and Sophie."

"My cousin is the most empty-headed fellow," said the marquess. "And his wife is the most hen-witted creature. I did not expect them about in the morning."

Before Olivia could launch into a defense of Aubrey and Sophie, the two of them entered the room. "Good morning, Livy," said Lady Roxbury, greeting Olivia with a kiss on the cheek. She then smiled at Lord Branford. "Edward, how well you look."

The marquess nodded. "And so do you, Sophie."

Aubrey shook his cousin's hand vigorously. "How do, cousin? And where is your lovely wife?"

"At the milliner's."

"A pity," said Aubrey, "but it is so good to see you, old man. It has been so long since we've had a proper chat."

"That is true," said the marquess, "however, I fear, Aubrey, that I must rush off. I am to meet Colonel Amesbury about buying a horse."

Aubrey was very interested. "A horse?"

The marquess nodded.

"I do wish I could go with you, Edward," said the baronet disappointedly, "but Sophie and I have an appointment."

"Perhaps another time," said Lord Branford, trying to hide his relief at not having to have his cousin accompany him. He hastily took his leave.

"Colonel Amesbury has had some fine horses," said Aubrey, escorting his wife to the sofa and then sitting down beside her. "I shall never forget Vulcan's Forge and how he could jump."

"Aubrey, I beg you not to speak of horses!" cried Sophie. "We are here to see Olivia." She looked over at her friend. "My dear, you do not appear in the best of tempers. I do hope you and Edward were not quarreling."

"I suppose we were," replied Olivia.

"Oh dear," said Aubrey. "What was it about?"

"I asked my brother if I might set up my own establishment, just a small place in town. Edward would not hear of it."

"My poor Livy," said Sophie sympathetically. "But we have come with the solution to your problem. We want you to come with us to the country."

"Oh, yes," said Aubrey, "you must do so. We are going to Northumberland at the end of the month."

"Northumberland!" replied Olivia in some surprise.

"Oh, I did not want to go," said Sophie. "Indeed, I preferred our house in Surrey. However, Aubrey is adamant about the north country. He cannot stop talking about the Malvern Hunt. I am certain that Northumberland will be quite barbarous, especially after meeting Lord Ramsay."

"Then why on earth are you going?"

"Because I wish it," said Sir Aubrey with a grin, "and I am the master, after all."

"What nonsense," said Olivia. "I daresay, Sophie, you decided to go, but I cannot understand why."

Sophie smiled. "I must say I was very curious to see Fenwyck and this dreadful castle of Ramsay's. I think it would be such an adventure. And besides that, it will be perfect for you to have enough time to win the wager. A fortnight in town might not be quite long enough for a man like that to come to his senses. This morning we discussed the idea and decided it would be quite the thing."

"My dear Sophie," said Olivia, "don't you think this wager has gone too far?"

"Certainly not," returned the other young lady. "It has only just begun. I cannot wait to see Ramsay again."

"Well, I do not think you will have that opportunity. The baron is not a very sociable person. I doubt he'll call upon you."

"Don't be a goose, Livy," said Sophie. "Of course he won't call upon us. We must call upon him, and do so right at once."

Aubrey nodded. "It is all arranged. I have already discovered where the baron is staying, the Halliburton Arms in Bloomsbury. I daresay I would not stay in Bloomsbury myself, nor would I normally visit anyone there, but I shall make an exception in this case."

"Is it not exciting, Olivia?" said Sophie. "We will go to Ramsay's hotel for luncheon. I think it very daring to do so, since it is so unfashionable. My dear, it is patronized by provincial shopkeepers! If you marry Ramsay, you must not allow him to stay at such places."

Olivia laughed at her friend's prattle. "You are ridiculous, Sophie!"

Aubrey pulled his watch from his pocket. "I do think we should be off. Are you ready to go, Livy?"

"Indeed, I am not. I don't think this is a very good idea. You cannot think Ramsay will wish a visit from us?"

"I'm dashed if I know why he should not," said Aubrey. "I'm sure he will think it a great kindness for us to do so. Now, hurry, and get ready, cousin. It grows late."

Olivia hesitated for a moment and then gave in. "Very well," she said, smiling at them both, "but if it is a disaster, I shall blame you." Then she left them and hurried up to her room to change.

The Halliburton Arms was a respectable establishment with a prosperous middle-class clientele. Its owner, Mr. Channing, was wealthy and successful, but despite his good fortune, he often regretted that his hotel was not frequented by members of the aristocracy.

Therefore, Mr. Channing was quite thrilled to see a gentleman dressed at the height of fashion, accompanied by two lovely and equally stylish ladies, enter his door. Hurrying to meet these obvious persons of quality, Channing bowed obsequiously. "How may I help you, sir?"

Aubrey smiled condescendingly. "We are here to call upon Lord Ramsay." He plucked a calling card from his pocket and handed it to Mr. Channing. "Do tell his lordship that Lady Roxbury and Lady Olivia are here as well."

The hotel owner looked down at the gilt-edged card and then at Sir Aubrey with a befuddled expression. "I am sorry, Sir Aubrey, but there is no Lord Ramsay staying here."

"Egad, man, I was told he was here," drawled Aubrey, eyeing the man with his quizzing glass. "Perhaps you might be so good as to check your register."

"Very well, sir," replied Mr. Channing. "I shall check with my assistant."

While the hotel owner went to confer with an another man, Sophie looked around the lobby. "Why, this is very nice. I expected it to be quite tawdry."

"I am sorry you are disappointed," said Olivia, smiling at her friend.

"Well, it is hardly exciting," returned Lady Roxbury. "And now it appears that Lord Ramsay is not even staying here. I fear your information was wrong, Aubrey."

The baronet shook his head. "I cannot understand it. I thought my information reliable."

At that moment Mr. Channing returned. "Sir Aubrey, we have no Lord Ramsay registered. However, there is a Mr. Ramsay from Tynborough."

"Tynborough? Why, that is the village near Hawkesmuir Castle. It must be Ramsay. Is he a man with dark hair and a slight limp?"

Mr. Channing had to consult with his assistant once again. "Yes, sir, he is."

"Then that is the gentleman we want. Do tell him we are here."

"My assistant informs me that Mr. . . . I should say, Lord Ramsay has gone out. He is expected back in an hour or so."

Sir Aubrey looked a little disappointed, but then brightened. "That should do very nicely. We will have luncheon here and wait for him." The baronet looked at the hotel owner. "If you can accommodate us, Mr. . . . ."

"Channing, sir, and I shall be most honored to do so. If you and the ladies will please follow me."

Mr. Channing led them to the hotel restaurant and was most solicitous in securing the best table for his illustrious visitors. The other patrons of the restaurant were most interested in seeing members of the *haut ton* among them and kept directing curious glances toward their table, much to Olivia's amusement. Sophie and Aubrey did not seem to notice the attention they were receiving, so intent were they on the luncheon.

"I say," said the baronet, eating heartily. "I have never had chops to compare with these. Pity they don't have a chef like this at my club."

"It is a pity we don't have him at our home, my dear," said Sophie, taking a forkful of salmon. "The food is wonderful. We must tell everyone about it."

They had completed their delicious repast when Mr. Channing returned to their table. "Channing," said the baronet, "the food was deuced good. My compliments to your chef."

The hotel owner beamed at the remark, but then looked a trifle uneasy. "Lord Ramsay has returned, sir," he said.

"Did you tell him we were here?"

"I did, sir."

"Is he joining us?" asked Aubrey.

"I fear not, sir," said Channing. "He has gone out again."

"The devil!" cried the baronet. "Without a word to us?"

"He did send his regrets, sir."

"The audacity of the man," said Sophie indignantly.

Olivia laughed. "Oh dear, we have frightened him off."

Aubrey frowned. "He must have had an important appointment." He looked up at the hotel owner. "Did he say where he was going?"

Channing cleared his throat. "He inquired about a toy shop, sir. We told him there was a very fine shop nearby. It is called Finch's. I think he was going there."

"A toy shop," said Sophie incredulously. "So that is his important business!"

Olivia laughed again. "It is too funny. Shall we not follow him there?"

"Yes, that is a good idea," said the baronet. After settling his bill very generously and receiving directions on how to get to the toy shop, Sir Aubrey, accompanied by the ladies, left the hotel.

As the shop was only a few blocks distant, the baronet instructed his driver to meet them there and they began walking down the street. "I was just quizzing you when I said that we should follow the baron," said Olivia, very amused by the situation.

"No, I think we should find him," said Aubrey.

"Indeed, yes," said Sophie. "I do wonder why he is going to a toy shop. I find this baron very mysterious, and I do not like mysteries overmuch."

"Nor do I," said Aubrey. "I think it also dashed peculiar that the fellow would not have used his title at that hotel. What is the point of having a title if one does not use it! And the gall of him to snub us! I should like to give him a piece of my mind!"

"But do not forget the wager, cousin," said Olivia, trying to maintain a straight face.

"No, no, I shall not," replied the baronet.

Soon they arrived at the window of the toy shop and all three peered inside. There was the baron intently scrutinizing a model of a ship. "There he is," cried Sophie. "Should we go in and see him?"

"Oh, Sophie," replied Olivia. "I should be too embarrassed."

Three stylishly dressed and obviously well-to-do personages staring into a toy-shop window created some interest on the narrow street of shops. Several passersby regarded them curiously, and some glanced into the toy shop, thinking there must be something very unusual inside.

Olivia was amused by the way Ramsay went from toy to

toy, studying each with great care and a somber expression. He finally settled upon a knight on a horse fashioned from tin.

"He is finally buying something," said Sophie. "It takes me less time to buy a hat."

"I don't think he is nearly so accustomed to buying things as you, my dear," said Aubrey.

Lady Roxbury cast a warning look at her husband, who smiled.

"Oh, he is coming," said Olivia. "We must not let him see us."

As the baron took up his parcel and turned toward the shop door, the three scurried away and ran into the shop next door. The proprietor of this establishment, a bookseller, was rather surprised to see them. "Might I assist you, ladies and sir?"

"What?" said Aubrey, watching out the window of the bookshop and catching sight of Ramsay walking in their direction. All three snatched up books and placed them in front of their faces as the baron passed by.

Olivia peeked over her book. "There he goes," she said. "I think we are safe."

The bookseller regarded them in bewilderment. "May I be of assistance?" he repeated.

"I shall take this book," said Aubrey, handing the volume he was holding to the bookseller.

The man took it and glanced down at the title. "*The Ladies' Guide to Household Management*. A good choice, sir."

"Indeed, yes," said the baronet, smiling at his wife.

That lady, however, was not attending. She and Olivia were watching Ramsay stride down the street. "We must follow him, Aubrey."

"Of course, my dear," said the baronet, hastily producing a coin and giving it to the bookseller. They rushed out before Aubrey could collect his change, leaving the bookshop owner to shake his head at the ways of the nobility.

Once outside on the street, Aubrey waved to his waiting carriage driver. "We shall follow him in the carriage."

Olivia, who was thoroughly enjoying herself, eagerly climbed up into the equipage. "Oh, this is such fun," she said. "I should have died if Ramsay had seen us in the bookshop."

Sophie laughed. "Was it not too funny?" She looked out the window. "He is walking very fast. Indeed, we could never keep up with him on foot. It is quite remarkable for a man with a limp." Looking over at her husband, Lady Roxbury noted he was carrying a book. "What is that, Aubrey?"

"A book, my dear. I bought it just now."

"How quickly you do things," said Sophie. "I do hope it is a gift for me. I would love a new novel."

The baronet handed the volume to her and grinned. "I am certain you will enjoy it."

Lady Roxbury opened the book eagerly and glanced at the title page. "Household management? Aubrey!"

Sir Aubrey laughed. "I thought it looked deuced interesting."

"Then you can read it, Aubrey," said his wife. "I assure you, I shall not."

"Then we had best give it to Livy as a wedding present," returned the baronet.

"Indeed, yes," said Sophie, handing the book to her friend. "It will be of use to you when you reside at Hawkesmuir Castle." They all laughed, and the carriage continued on its way.

4

The pursuit of Baron Ramsay led Olivia, Aubrey, and Sophie to an impressive-looking building less than a mile from the toy shop. The carriage came to a halt some distance away and they looked out the window to watch the baron make his way inside the edifice.

"Why, it appears he is calling on someone," said Sir Aubrey. "I can't imagine whom a person would know in Bloomsbury. Why, look, there are others going inside! 'Pon my honor, whoever lives here is receiving a good many callers."

Olivia burst into laughter. "Oh, Aubrey, that is the British Museum."

"The devil you say!" returned the baronet. "He is going there?"

"I am told some think it an interesting place," said Sophie dubiously.

"Well, I think we should go in," said Olivia.

"Indeed, yes." Sophie nodded vigorously. "I daresay this baron is becoming even more mysterious. We must discover what he is doing here."

"I am sure he is just seeing the exhibits," suggested Olivia.

"So he would rather see a bunch of old fossils than us," said Aubrey, frowning.

Olivia laughed. "Perhaps he is just showing good judgment, cousin."

Aubrey grinned and assisted the ladies from the carriage. They proceeded to the British Museum, and once inside the portals of this august institution, they glanced curiously about the vast entry hall with its huge staircase and brightly decorated walls. "I do not see Ramsay," said Sophie.

"Come, let us go up," said Aubrey, offering his arms to the ladies.

They ascended the stairs and were met at the landing by a short bespectacled man. "Welcome, ladies and sir," he said. "Do follow me. Your guide will be with you shortly."

Aubrey started to say that they did not want a guide, but Sophie nudged him into silence. They followed the man into a handsome saloon furnished with a curious collection of museum artifacts. "You will find many interesting items here, I am sure," said the man, "and your guide will join you in a moment."

After he had left them, Aubrey shook his head. "I daresay I had no intention of spending the afternoon looking at musty exhibits."

Sophie started to wander about the room. She stopped suddenly in front of a glass case. "But look at this, Aubrey, a mummy! It is quite horrid!"

"Good God," said the baronet, following his wife's gaze and lifting his quizzing glass to his eye. "It is a mummy!"

"And you thought it would be dull, Aubrey," said Olivia. "I have never seen a mummy before and I am sure we will be the envy of everyone for having seen one."

"Well, I think it ghastly," said Aubrey, "and scarcely the sort of thing that should be viewed by ladies." After staring at the mummy for some time, the three of them turned their attention to the other artifacts on display. They included various specimens of coral, a vulture's head in spirits, and a stuffed flamingo. These objects so engrossed Olivia and her friends that it hardly seemed that any time had passed before the guide entered the room.

A tall, balding, and congenial-looking gentleman approached them. "I am Mr. Caruthers. I shall escort you about the museum."

"I say, Caruthers," said the baronet, "don't you think that mummy a trifle gruesome for ladies?"

Mr. Caruthers smiled. "Indeed, sir, the ladies love all the Egyptian antiquities, especially the mummies."

"Don't be silly, Aubrey," said Olivia, "I assure you that the poor creature will cause no one to have an attack of the vapors."

Although Sir Aubrey did not appear to be entirely convinced, he said nothing further as Mr. Caruthers led them from the saloon to the department of manuscripts to admire the Magna Carta. They then proceeded to rooms full of geological specimens. Aubrey found rocks and minerals very dull and was happy when Caruthers led them into another large room with many glass cases. "Oh," said Sophie distastefully as she glanced down at one of the cases, "they are insects! I detest insects!"

"My, my," said Aubrey, "there are a dashed lot of them." He peered at the specimens through his quizzing glass. " 'Pon my soul, look at that beetle! And the jaws on it! I daresay I should not like to find that fellow in my boot!"

"How dreadful," said Sophie. "Mr. Caruthers, I hope there are other exhibits more suitable to a lady's interests."

"Indeed so, ma'am," replied Caruthers. "I shall take you now to the historical artifacts. They are always a favorite with the ladies." The baronet seemed rather reluctant to leave the insects, but acquiesced. They made their way to the historical exhibits and were so interested in them that they quite forgot about looking for Ramsay.

"I must tell the gentlemen at the club about this," said

Sir Aubrey, eyeing an ax from an ancient Celtic village. "Why, one would have thought this place would be awfully flat, but it is dashed interesting."

Sophie was not as enthusiastic. "It seems there are too many swords and battleaxes for my taste, but I must say it is not nearly so dull as I imagined."

Olivia laughed. "But I think we have forgotten the original purpose in coming here. I would have thought we might have found him among the suits of armor."

Mr. Caruthers regarded her with interest. "Were you looking for someone, ma'am?"

"We did hope to see a friend of ours," replied Olivia.

"Yes," said Aubrey. "His name is . . . Mr. Ramsay. He has dark hair and walks with a slight limp. Might you have seen him, Caruthers?"

"You must mean Lord Ramsay of Hawkesmuir, sir," replied Caruthers.

"Confound him," muttered the baronet, "why is he not consistent? Have you seen Lord Ramsay, then?"

"I have not, sir, but perhaps he is in the reading room. He is a scholar."

"Scholar?" said Aubrey. "I don't know about that. He is a gentleman."

"Where is the reading room, Mr. Caruthers?" asked Olivia, noting that their guide was eyeing Aubrey with something akin to disapproval.

"It is through that corridor, ma'am."

Aubrey thanked Caruthers for the excellent tour and then he and the ladies departed for the reading room. "It does seem likely that Ramsay would be in such a place," said the baronet. "Malvern said he was quite mad about books."

Arriving at the entrance of the reading room, they found it guarded by an officious-looking man dressed in rather shabby clothes. He regarded them first with surprise and then disapproval. Obviously unaccustomed to finding an embodiment of dandyism standing before him, the man frowned at Sir Aubrey's sartorial splendor, noting the baronet's exquisitely cut olive coat and bright yellow pantaloons. Aubrey's neckcloth was tied in a magnificent waterfall and his bright red curls were modishly coiffed in the Corinthian style. "May I help you?" said the man ill-humoredly.

"Yes" said Sir Aubrey. "We are looking for Lord Ramsay of Hawkesmuir, a dark-haired man with a limp. He's frightfully bookish."

Since the other gentleman was a librarian, this comment elicited a frown upon his dour countenance. "I am well acquainted with his lordship," said the librarian. "He is at work and I am sure he would not wish to be disturbed."

"But we are friends of Lord Ramsay, sir," said Olivia, smiling sweetly at the man. "I know he would be very happy to see us, even though I am sure he is engaged in some very important work."

Her famous smile had the desired effect and the librarian's face softened. "He is, ma'am. At present he is studying *The Hour Book of Baron de Courcy*. It is one of our rarest medieval manuscripts. The illuminations are quite extraordinary."

"How very fascinating," said Olivia. "Perhaps it would be very rude of us to disrupt him."

The librarian smiled at Olivia. "I am certain that his lordship would think me very remiss if I did not allow you to see him. Of course, I must tell you that usually one cannot be admitted to the reading room without formal application to the trustees."

"Egad," muttered Aubrey, "it is probably easier to get into Almack's."

The librarian ignored the baronet and smiled again at Olivia. "I shall make an exception and allow you in."

"How kind of you, sir," said Olivia, once again directing her well-known smile at the man.

As they entered the reading room, Sophie whispered to

her friend, "It is a pity that fellow was not Ramsay. He would be offering for you before the day is out."

Olivia laughed and the ladies and Aubrey proceeded across the silent library. They spied the baron seated at a long table, intent upon a large book. Pausing, they watched him study a page from the manuscript and then make rapid notes with a pencil on some paper beside the book. After exchanging glances, Sir Aubrey and the ladies continued toward him.

"Lord Ramsay," said Aubrey.

The baron looked up and appeared so startled at the sight of the three of them that he dropped his pencil. "Roxbury?" he said, rising to his feet.

"Is this not the most dashed amazing coincidence to find you here?" said Sir Aubrey.

"Coincidence?" repeated Ramsay, raising his dark eyebrows skeptically.

"Why, yes," said the baronet. "Of course, we called on you at your hotel, but you were not in. Since we were in Bloomsbury, Lady Olivia insisted we come to the British Museum."

The baron directed a look at Olivia as if for confirmation of this remark. Olivia tried not to laugh. "Yes," she said, "whenever I am in Bloomsbury, I do not miss the opportunity to come here."

Thinking he detected irony in the lady's blue eyes, Ramsay frowned slightly. "So you often come to the reading room, Lady Olivia?"

"That she does, Lord Ramsay," said Sophie. "Olivia is so bookish. Indeed, she is quite the bluestocking. I am always telling her to quit reading so much. She might ruin her lovely eyes!"

Ramsay's expression told Olivia he considered Sophie's remark complete humbug. "I see you are a scholar, my lord," said Olivia. "Why, is that not *The Hour Book of Baron de Courcy*? The illuminations are quite extraordinary."

The baron regarded her in surprise. "Yes, that is what it is. You are familiar with it, ma'am?"

"Oh yes," interjected Sophie, "Olivia has read it many times. She always talks about it. Indeed, I tire of hearing about this Baron de Courcy."

Olivia directed a warning look at her friend. Glancing back at Ramsay, she noted that a slight smile had appeared on the baron's face. "So you read Norman French, Lady Olivia?" he said. "Perhaps you might assist me with my translation."

"Oh, I would not presume to do so, Lord Ramsay," said Olivia hastily. "I assure you I am no scholar."

"You are too modest, Livy," said Aubrey. He grinned at Ramsay. "Why, were my cousin a man, I daresay she would be an Oxford don."

This remark was so ludicrous that Olivia could not refrain from laughter. This unaccustomed noise caused several scholarly-looking gentlemen sitting in the reading room to regard them with disapproval. "Lord Ramsay," said Olivia, "I fear my cousin is quite ridiculous."

"I am not at all," said Aubrey, directing a broad grin at the baron. "I say, you do look busy, Ramsay. I fear that we are disrupting your work and you'd like us to leave."

"You are, actually," said the baron matter-of-factly, "and the reading room is hardly the place for conversation."

Rather taken aback by Ramsay's rudeness, Sir Aubrey looked startled.

Olivia was also surprised and irked by the baron's un-civil response. "We should not keep his lordship from his work," she said stiffly. "We must go."

Ramsay, noting the coolness of Olivia's remarks, sud-denly regretted his words. Before he could say anything, Sophie intervened. "We cannot go before I invite you to Roxbury House for dinner tomorrow evening." Both Olivia and Aubrey looked at Lady Roxbury in surprise. She continued. "Do say you'll come."

The baron regarded Sophie as if he had not heard correctly. "Dinner at your house tomorrow?"

"I know it is very sudden invitation, but I hope you will overlook that, Lord Ramsay," said Sophie, smiling sweetly at him. "Lady Olivia will be there, of course, but it is just a small, intimate gathering."

The baron had not expected this and it took him a few moments to collect his thoughts. "Lady Roxbury, I don't think I—"

"My dear sir, you may not refuse me without incurring my wrath," said Sophie. "You cannot disappoint us."

The baron was not a man who could be badgered into doing anything, and he was tempted to give Lady Roxbury a firm refusal. However, the recollection of his earlier discourtesy and Olivia's displeasure checked him. "Very well, Lady Roxbury, I shall come."

"Splendid, Lord Ramsay," cried Sophie.

"Then let us not bother his lordship any longer," said Olivia. "Good day to you, sir."

"Good day," returned Ramsay.

Sophie and Aubrey murmured their farewells and then they followed Olivia away. The baron watched them go, a perplexed expression on his face. When they had left the reading room, he sat down again.

Why in the world would they follow him and invite him to dinner? he asked himself. Knitting his brows in concentration, Ramsay cynically arrived at the answer. It was obvious that Lady Olivia was in search of a husband. It was not the first time that he had been pursued for his wealth. Indeed, in Northumberland all manner of ambitious matrons thought him a prize for their daughters.

The baron frowned as he thought of the beautiful Lady Olivia. He knew about women of that type. Her aristocratic family was undoubtedly ruined by profligate spending and she was having difficulty paying for all the gowns she needed for attending silly balls. Frivolous and emptyheaded, a woman like Lady Olivia would do anything to

ensnare a rich man, even pretend an interest in books. Of
course, thought Ramsay, it was rather odd that she knew
about the de Courcy manuscript.

Momentarily puzzled by this face, the baron thought of
the dinner invitation. He cursed himself for accepting it.
The idea of sitting at the dinner table with fops and fortune
huntresses was not at all appealing. Thinking of Sir Aubrey's fashionable attire, Ramsay shook his head. The
fellow was preposterous, he told himself. It was obvious
he had not a brain in his head, and his wife was another of
those detestable females who thought a pretty face was
enough to secure everyone's good opinion.

The baron looked down at the manuscript on the table
and frowned again. He tried to work awhile longer, but
after a short time he found it was useless to continue. His
mind could not concentrate on the medieval manuscript.
To his irritation, all he could think of was Lady Olivia and
her confounded beauty.

Ramsay collected his notes and the parcel he had obtained at the toy shop and ill-humoredly rose from his seat.
Leaving the reading room, he addressed the officious librarian. "I am done for today, Sloan."

"Very good, my lord. We will have the manuscript
ready for you again tomorrow if you wish."

The baron nodded. "I shall return in the morning."

Ramsay turned to go, but the librarian stopped him with
a question. "My lord?"

"Yes, Sloan?"

"I do hope your lordship is not annoyed with me for
directing the gentleman and ladies to you. I thought your
lordship would wish to see them."

"You directed them?"

He nodded. "I am sorry, but they seemed most eager to
find you."

Ramsay looked very interested. "They were looking for
me here?"

"Yes, my lord. I told them you were looking at *The Book of Hours of Baron de Courcy*."

"And did you tell them that the illuminations were extraordinary?"

"I believe I did, my lord."

To the librarian's surprise, the baron burst out laughing. "I'm damned," said Ramsay. "That explains the lady's knowledge."

"My lord?"

"Nothing, Sloan. No, you did nothing wrong in directing the visitors to me. I daresay you could not have kept the ladies from their purpose in any case. Good day, Sloan."

The librarian regarded the baron quizzically and then bowed slightly. As the baron exited the reading room, another gentleman hurried out after him. "I say, Lord Ramsay!"

His lordship turned to face a man with whom he was slightly and unfavorably acquainted. "Hedgewood," he said coolly.

The man who stood before him was stout and red-faced, but dressed with more than the usual scholar's care. Ramsay knew he had some claim to being a historian, although the baron thought his scholarship mediocre and his writing unreadable. Having met Hedgewood on a few occasions, the baron disliked his fawning, ingratiating manner.

"Was that not Sir Aubrey Roxbury I saw speaking to you?"

"It was."

"And Lady Roxbury and Lady Olivia Dunbar?"

Ramsay raised an eyebrow and frowned. "You are acquainted with them?"

"Alas, no, my lord, although I have seen them from afar, you might say. Why, everyone knows of Sir Aubrey and his lady. And Lady Olivia! By Jove, she is the most beautiful woman in the kingdom! By God, you are a lucky fellow to have her interested in you." Although the baron's expression was now icy, Hedgewood did not seem to notice. He continued. "And not only is she the loveliest creature, but Lady Olivia is an heiress. It will be a fortunate man who will wed her."

"An heiress! What do you mean?"

Hedgewood appeared surprised that the baron was unaware of this information. "She is not precisely an heiress, I suppose, but it is a well-known fact that her marriage settlement is enormous. Her brother is the Marquess of Branford, you know. She is the most-sought-after woman in town. Why, she has refused so many suitors that she is called Lady *No*livia!" Hedgewood grinned, but quickly eased his smile as he noted that Ramsay was not in the least amused.

"Do excuse me, Hedgewood," said the baron. "I must be going." Not allowing the talkative gentleman another word, Ramsay walked off, a thoughtful expression on his face.

5

Olivia sat at her dressing table, studying herself in the mirror while her maid fastened a garland of white roses in her hair. "Oh, m'lady, you look lovely," said the servant.

"Thank you, Hannah. That will be all." The maid curtsied and left.

Olivia frowned as she continued to stare pensively into the mirror. One would have thought a lady who looked as splendid as she did at that moment would have appeared far happier, but Olivia seemed oblivious of the lovely picture she presented. She was attired in a stunning white satin gown with a very low neckline and high waist. Her golden hair was dressed in the French style with a profusion of full curls at the sides of her face.

Olivia was not looking forward to dinner at the Roxburys' that evening, knowing that Ramsay would be there. Certainly Sophie had carried the joke too far by inviting the baron. Olivia frowned again as she remembered seeing him at the British Museum the day before. He had been very rude and apparently had nothing but contempt for them.

Olivia sighed and rose from the dressing table. Taking

up her white kid gloves, she made her way downstairs. She entered the drawing room and found her brother, Edward, and Jocasta seated there. Edward was dressed in fashionable evening clothes and Jocasta wore a modish rose-colored gown. "So you are ready finally," said Jocasta.

Olivia ignored her sister-in-law's quarrelsome tone. "How well you both look," she said.

"And you look simply marvelous, Livy," said Edward. "I do wish you were going with us. I think it would have been better for you to accompany us to the Claridges'. I still do not approve of your going to a dinner party at Aubrey's on such short notice."

"It is so like Sophie to be so ramshackle as to arrange a dinner party at the last second," commented Jocasta. "But I know well that Olivia prefers the Roxburys' company to any other."

Olivia held her tongue and Edward spoke. "We must be going if we are to take you to Aubrey's." Olivia nodded, and her brother escorted her and Jocasta from the room.

Baron Ramsay wound his linen neckcloth around his collar and tied it in a simple knot. Noting the result of his efforts in the mirror, his lordship smiled slightly. How different his cravat was from Sir Aubrey Roxbury's extravagantly tied creation. Doubtless that gentleman or his valet had spent an inordinate amount of time fashioning the preposterous thing, he thought.

The baron turned away and picked up his coat from the bed and slipped it on. It was several seasons old and the work of an inferior village tailor. Ramsay glanced into the mirror and frowned. Usually he did not care one fig for the cut of his evening clothes. Indeed, he had only disdain for fashion, thinking it the province of idiots.

However, tonight the idea of being thought poorly dressed and ridiculous by the Roxburys and Lady Olivia was not particularly pleasing. It crossed his mind briefly that he should spend some time in London at one of the well-known tailors'. Promptly rejecting the idea, the baron told himself not to be a fool. He had far more important things to do than gad about town buying clothes like a deuced dandy.

The baron looked in the mirror again and eyed himself critically. He could not deny that he looked dreadfully shabby, and he reconsidered his resolution not to waste time on a London tailor. Perhaps it would not take very long to be fitted for new clothes, he reflected, deciding to visit a tailor after all.

Ramsay walked across the room and stared out into the darkened London streets. He wondered about Lady Olivia and her friends and why they had asked him to dinner. The baron had been so certain that Olivia was a scheming fortune huntress that the information that she was wealthy had totally confused him. Although he had given much thought to the subject, he had been unable to come up with any other explanation for her interest in him.

Ramsay frowned again. It must be some kind of joke, he decided glumly. Surely at this moment they were laughing at his expense, thinking him so very amusing and eccentric. Hardly cheered by these reflections, Ramsay turned away from the window. Then, throwing his well-worn cloak around his shoulders and taking up his cane and beaver hat, he left the room.

To the baron's considerable irritation, the hotel owner, Mr. Channing, met him in the lobby. "Your lordship!" he cried loudly, and Ramsay saw every head turn in his direction. "Your lordship is going out?"

"I am," returned the baron, directing a dark look at the man and silently cursing Sir Aubrey for revealing his identity. When he came to London, the baron always stayed at the Halliburton Arms because of it proximity to the British Museum. Not wishing special attention, he preferred the anonymity of being plain Mr. Ramsay. It was now especially irksome having the hotel's owner and all its staff toady to him.

"May I assist you, my lord?" said Channing eagerly.

"No, you may not," said the baron testily, hurrying out of the lobby. The hotel owner did not seem to mind, but smiled in a long-suffering fashion as if he were well accustomed to lordly privilege and temper.

Olivia said little on the short ride to her cousin's house and was glad that neither Edward nor Jocasta made any further comments about the Roxburys. She was rather relieved when Edward deposited her on Aubrey's doorstep and the Roxburys' efficient butler admitted her into the stylishly appointed drawing room.

As always, Olivia was rather amused at the decoration of this room. It was very large and its walls were painted a fashionable sky blue with an intricately painted geometric border of sea green and gold near the ceiling. Sophie had hoped to create a stylishly exotic effect, as evidenced by the Oriental furniture and Persian carpets. However, since Aubrey had refused to have his favorite paintings removed from the walls, the portraits of horses and hounds had remained, giving the room a curious incongruous appearance.

Sophie and Aubrey soon joined Olivia in the drawing room. "Livy!" cried Lady Roxbury. "You look ravishing! I daresay Lord Ramsay can scarcely be indifferent to you this evening."

"If he is," said Aubrey, "he is a very odd fish indeed."

"He is an odd fish, Aubrey," said Olivia, smiling at them. "And I fancy my new gown will be lost on him."

"Then you may have to resort to your knowledge of medieval manuscripts, my dear," said Sophie, directing a mischievous smile at her friend.

"Do not make me laugh," cried Olivia. "And I pray that neither of you mentions that de Courcy book or whatever it was called."

"Very well," said Sophie, "but I am counting on you to charm our guest. It appears he is not easily charmed, so it will be a challenge for you."

They sat down and talked, and after some time had passed, Olivia began to wonder if Ramsay would appear. The same thought occurred to Aubrey. "He is dashed late," muttered the baronet, looking over at the mantel clock. "Cook will be in a lather if we do not dine soon."

"Oh, Cook has braved far worse than this, my dear," said Sophie, seemingly unconcerned. "Do not fear, Lord Ramsay will arrive shortly."

She had scarcely said these words when the butler entered and announced Baron Ramsay. They all turned toward the door and waited with eager anticipation until his lordship appeared.

Olivia could not fail to note Ramsay's sorry attire, his ill-fitting old-fashioned coat and knee breeches and carelessly tied neckcloth. He had a wild look about him that seemed ill-suited to the Roxburys' drawing room.

"I am sorry I am late," he said.

"My dear baron," said Sophie, "you are scarcely late, and there is no need to apologize."

Ramsay looked at the Roxburys and Olivia. "I see that I am not the last to arrive in any case," he said.

"I am afraid you are, Ramsay," said Aubrey, getting to his feet. "We have no other guests this evening."

"It is just the four of us," explained Sophie. "I know it is a terribly small dinner party, but I am so weary of large gatherings, aren't you, Lord Ramsay?"

"Very weary," replied the baron, supressing a smile. In truth, Ramsay seldom attended gatherings large or otherwise. His usual dinner company included only himself and two others. Although he was surprised to see no other guests, he was rather glad of it. He did not enjoy society, and the fewer people at a gathering, the better it suited him.

"I do think we should go in to dinner," said Sophie. "Shall we, Lord Ramsay?"

The baron replied with a slight bow and offered his arm to Lady Roxbury. Aubrey and Olivia exchanged a glance, and then, arm in arm, followed Ramsay and Sophie into the dining room.

It did strike Olivia as a trifle peculiar having so few at the massive cherry table, for she knew that at most times Sophie considered twenty guests a small dinner party. As they all took their seats clustered around one end of the table, Olivia had further misgivings about the evening. She was sitting between Aubrey and the baron, with Sophie across the table from her, and she feared she would have total responsibility for Ramsay's conversation. However, Sophie's chattering soon put this fear to rest.

Olivia could not fail to note that the baron seemed very ill-at-ease. He resisted Sophie's attempts to draw him into the conversation, but since the discussion centered chiefly on people he did not know and occasions he had not attended, this was not unusual.

It was not until the second course was laid before them that Olivia had the opportunity to turn the conversation to his lordship. "Lord Ramsay, we have been told you are a distinguished scholar. Why don't you tell us about your work?"

"I don't wish to bore you," returned the baron.

"Bore us?" said Sir Aubrey between forkfuls of stuffed haddock. "It's dashed interesting for a gentleman to be a scholar. What is it about those old musty books you find so dashed fascinating, Ramsay?"

"It is most difficult to explain to anyone who does not find them fascinating." He looked over at Olivia. "I'm sure that Lady Olivia would understand."

"Oh, yes," said Sophie, "Olivia shares your interest. How similar you are." Olivia and Ramsay regarded each other dubiously. Noting their expressions, Lady Roxbury changed the subject. "How very lucky we met you at Lord and Lady Digby's. Are you well acquainted with Digby, Lord Ramsay?"

"We are distantly related, ma'am," said the baron, "and therefore I am obliged to visit him when in town."

"We all have our duties, my lord," said Olivia with mock solemnity, and Ramsay frowned.

Fearing that Olivia and Ramsay were not getting along, Sophie again directed the conversation elsewhere. "I was so happy to meet you, Lord Ramsay, since we are to be neighbors in Northumberland. I daresay we shall be seeing a great deal of each other."

Olivia almost laughed at the expression this remark elicited from the baron's dark countenance. She was beginning to enjoy herself now that she had given up on the idea of being charming to Ramsay. How could one be charming to such a man? He was completely humorless and obviously despised their company.

Olivia glanced over at Sophie and noted that that lady was working very hard to be pleasant to her guest. It appeared she still had hopes of winning her brother's absurd wager. Suppressing a smile, Olivia looked over at the baron. He was concentrating on the food, seeming to prefer it to the conversation. A mischievous impulse came to her. It would be very amusing to put this rude baron in his place. Indeed, from now on, she would take every opportunity to give him a setdown.

"Yes, Ramsay," said Sir Aubrey, unaware of his cousin's thoughts, "we shall be going north ourselves at the end of this month. I am so looking forward to it. Town is very well during the Season, but it is time to go to the country. Fenwyck is a splendid place, and what hunts there will be! I am having two wonderful hunters brought over from Ireland. I cannot wait to see the beasts! Ah, hunting season! There is no time like it!" In his enthusiasm, the baronet had again forgotten his guest's aversion to hunting. Ramsay's unsmiling face suddenly recalled it to mind. "But it is not only the hunting," Aubrey added hastily. "I am sure the society is quite pleasant. I know my wife will enjoy it, since it will make such a change from town. We have invited Lady Olivia to accompany us, but as yet she has not agreed. You must help us convince her to come." The baronet looked expectantly at Ramsay.

"Yes, Lord Ramsay," said Olivia with a mocking expression. "I'm sure your considerable powers of persuasion are more than adequate to convince me to go."

Ramsay looked at Olivia. He was well aware of the sarcasm in her voice and he was perplexed to realize that she was purposely trying to annoy him. "I fear you and Lady Roxbury may find it quite dull," said the baron.

"I did fear that, my lord," said Olivia, "and now you have confirmed my suspicions. I shall not go, for I have such a terror of dullness."

"Good heavens, Ramsay," said Aubrey, "I had hoped you would convince Livy to go. Indeed, now my wife may change her mind, and I have spent months persuading her."

"Oh, Aubrey, I am quite resolved to go. How bad of you, Lord Ramsay, to say you think Northumberland dull," said Sophie.

"You misconstrue my words, ma'am," replied the baron. "I do not find it dull, but I suspect you and Lady Olivia would find it so."

"But I am sure that your local society is quite delightful," said Sophie. "You must tell us all about it."

"I fear I have little part in local society, ma'am, and, therefore, can say little."

"But you must know everyone," persisted Sophie.

"I know everyone whom I wish to know," replied Ramsay.

"I daresay that is a very select company indeed, is it not, my lord?" Olivia directed an ironical smile at the baron, who frowned.

"I am certain you know Malvern," said Aubrey, hastening to join the discussion. "He is such a good fellow."

Ramsay scowled. "I do know him."

Noting the baron's response, which indicated his dislike of the man, Olivia smiled brightly at Ramsay. "Oh, my cousin was so very impressed with Mr. Malvern. He sounds like such a delightful gentleman. Perhaps I should go to Northumberland just to make his acquaintance."

Ramsay frowned ominously. "You need not travel such a distance, Lady Olivia, to meet men of Malvern's cut. There are plenty of them in London."

"Oh, I know there are many charming gentlemen in London," said Olivia, "but Mr. Malvern sounds especially fascinating. Is he married, Lord Ramsay?"

Sophie grew worried at Ramsay's expression, for the baron looked as if he were growing angry with her friend. To her relief, Ramsay replied evenly. "No, he is not married."

"Now I surely shall reconsider accompanying you, Aubrey." Olivia laughed.

Sophie hurried to steer the conversation away from Malvern, but whatever the topic, Olivia was maddeningly contrary. She seemed to be intent on antagonizing the baron, and that gentleman was reacting accordingly. Lady Roxbury was glad when the dinner finally ended and she and Olivia left the gentlemen to their port.

Once in the drawing room, Sophie demanded an explanation. "What are you about, Livy? Why do you persist in vexing Lord Ramsay? We shall never win the wager if you continue!"

Olivia burst into laughter. "Oh, Sophie, do give up that ridiculous wager. There is no hope of that gentleman ever becoming enamored of me, I assure you. My dear Sophie, the man is so insufferable that I could not bear to continue humoring him. It is far more amusing to vex him. Oh, did you see how he looked at me when I praised Malvern? It was too funny!"

Sophie broke into a smile. "It was funny, but I caution you, do not go too far. I suspect Lord Ramsay has a violent temper, which he appears to be on the verge of losing. Promise me you will behave yourself."

"Oh, very well, Sophie. He is your guest and future

neighbor. But you must promise me that you will forget all about this wager.''

"But I so wanted to best Reggie," insisted Lady Roxbury.

"My dear Sophie, you would not have bested him in any case.''

Sophie shrugged. "Oh, very well."

"Good," said Olivia, and the ladies continued their conversation.

The gentlemen did not linger long over their wine and soon joined Olivia and Sophie in the drawing room. Sophie continued to ask Ramsay about Northumberland, and that gentleman continued to give short and unsatisfactory answers. Since she had promised to behave herself, Olivia said very little, allowing Aubrey and Sophie to carry the conversation. After less than an hour had passed, the baron made his excuses and departed, leaving Olivia to explain to her cousin Aubrey the cause of her exasperating behavior.

6

Throughout the next three weeks Olivia thought occasionally of Baron Ramsay. It always amused her to think of him at the British Museum poring over some dusty manuscript. She wondered if he ever thought of her, but rejected the idea. Surely he did not, she decided. Although Aubrey and Sophie sometimes mentioned the baron, they had thankfully dropped the matter of the wager.

Now that the social season was ending, many were leaving town. There were fewer parties to attend and the weather was cool and rainy. Finding herself more in the company of her sister-in-law, Jocasta, Olivia was beginning to become depressed. She knew that Aubrey and Sophie would soon be leaving for the north, and she would miss them very much.

She was somewhat consoled by the prospect of going to Branford, the family's ancestral estate. Olivia had spent many happy childhood days there and she loved it dearly. She looked forward to seeing some old friends, who had spent the Season in the country, as well as walking with Mayflower along familiar wooded paths.

Ensconced on the sofa in her sitting room, the whippet Mayflower beside her, Olivia sat reading a book. It was an exceedingly dreary day and rain pelted against her window.

"There you are, Olivia," Jocasta entered the sitting room.

Olivia put down her book. "Hello, Jocasta," she said, smiling at her sister-in-law. Although things were not altogether well between them, Olivia and Jocasta had come to an uneasy truce. Olivia was taking great care to stay out of her sister-in-law's way, a fact that Jocasta could not help but notice. Still, the two were far from being friends, and Olivia continually wished that her brother had consented to allowing her to have her own house.

Jocasta sat down in a chair. "Olivia, I must tell you about our plans for going to the country."

"Oh, good, I shall be so happy to go to Branford. When will we be leaving?"

"I fear we are not going to Branford."

"Not going to Branford?"

Her sister-in-law nodded. "No, I have just written to my mother. We are going to Wessex to stay with my father, the duke."

Olivia tried to hide her dismay at Jocasta's words. She had stayed at her sister-in-law's parents' house once before and had been utterly miserable. Jocasta's family was even more difficult to tolerate than Jocasta herself. The duke and duchess were both insufferably proud and overbearing, and the idea of staying with them was dreadful. "Did Edward agree to go?"

Jocasta regarded her resentfully. "Of course he did. He was quite eager to go. We will be staying into the new year and then going to Branford. Christmas at my father's estate will be such fun. Everyone will be there, including a number of eligible gentlemen, Olivia. Indeed, I have written to my mother asking her assistance in producing suitable young men for you. I am sure she will find a good many of them. We are leaving in a week, so you must begin to think about packing." Olivia found herself speechless at this deplorable news, but she managed to nod.

"Well, I cannot stay," continued Lady Branford. "I must hurry and go to the dressmaker."

Jocasta smiled as she left the room, and Olivia frowned gloomily. "Oh, Mayflower," she said, "what are we to do? I so wanted to go to Branford. I do not know how I can endure Jocasta's family."

The whippet regarded her mistress sympathetically. After some time of unhappy reflection, Olivia looked up to see a maid enter the room. "Sir Aubrey and Lady Roxbury are here to see you, m'lady."

Olivia brightened. "I shall come down immediately, Mary." With Mayflower at her heels, Olivia hurried downstairs to greet her cousin and friend. "Thank heaven you are here," she cried, embracing first Sophie and then Aubrey.

"My dear girl," said Aubrey, "what is wrong?"

After telling them to be seated and then sitting down herself, Olivia sighed. "Oh, it is too horrible! Jocasta has just told me that we are not going to Branford. We are to go to Wessex instead, and stay with her parents."

"Good God!" said Aubrey. "Not the duke! There is no greater bore in the kingdom."

"Poor Livy," said Sophie, "I cannot abide the duchess myself."

"Nor can I, and what is worse is that Jocasta has written to her, asking her to find me a husband! Oh, why did I not accept Westbrook?"

"It appears the situation is most serious," said Aubrey gravely.

"And we are to stay until after the new year, more than two months!" added Olivia.

"You would never last that long," said Sophie. "Something must be done."

Aubrey nodded and appeared thoughtful for a moment. "I have it, Livy. You must go with us to Northumberland."

"Of course!" cried Sophie. "You cannot refuse to go

now. Surely even Fenwyck is better than the prospect of staying with the duke. Do say you'll come.''

''But I thought you were leaving tomorrow.''

''But it will not take you long to make ready,'' said Aubrey. ''And we shall be happy to delay our departure for you.''

''Certainly,'' said Sophie. ''Oh, it will be so much more fun if you come with us!''

Olivia considered the matter for only a moment. ''I will come! I am so grateful to you both.''

''Capital!'' cried Aubrey.

''Oh, yes!'' said Sophie excitedly, but then she looked as if she had just remembered something. ''Oh dear, I had quite forgotten your brother. I daresay Edward will not be very pleased about your coming with us. I do hope he will not prevent it.''

''My dear Sophie, Jocasta will be so glad that I am not accompanying them that she will convince Edward to allow me to go with you. You must help me to make ready, Sophie,'' said Olivia eagerly.

Aubrey rose to his feet. ''I see that I am not needed here. I shall leave you ladies to your work and return later.'' The baronet departed and Olivia and Sophie hurried up to Olivia's room, the whippet Mayflower following happily behind them.

7

On the same day that Olivia Dunbar decided to accompany the Roxburys to Northumberland, Gervas Ramsay, tenth Baron Ramsay of Hawkesmuir, arrived home. It was early evening and in the darkening sky Hawkesmuir Castle appeared a forbidding place. Indeed, even in the bright sunlight the castle's great stone walls had the aspect of a grim medieval fortress, and most would have thought approaching it at night rather daunting. However, the baron regarded the brooding edifice fondly as he walked up to its massive door.

The elderly servant who opened the giant door smiled at seeing the baron. "M'lord! We did not expect you for two days. What a welcome surprise, m'lord!"

"Thank you, Hardy," said Ramsay, smiling at the old man as he handed him his coat and hat. "It's damned good to be home."

Olivia would have been surprised to see the baron at that moment. He seemed completely transformed from the grim uncivil gentleman he appeared in town. His dark countenance was smiling and one would have thought him the most amiable of men.

There was a deep bark as Ramsay started across the entrance hall, and the baron grinned as a huge brindled dog bounded up to him. "Wolstan!" cried Ramsay, seemingly overjoyed to see the creature.

The dog, an enormous mastiff, could hardly contain his joy at seeing his master. His whole body quivered with excitement and he looked adoringly up at the baron. Ramsay laughed and took the dog's giant head between his hands. "So you have missed me, have you, brute?" The mastiff barked and the baron laughed again.

"Uncle Gervas!" A young boy dashed into the entrance hall and threw himself into Ramsay's outstretched arms. "You are back! I missed you so much!"

The baron hugged the lad tightly. "And I you, Geordie. Have you been a good boy while I've been gone?"

Geordie pulled away from Ramsay and grinned up at him. "I have, mostly." The boy glanced over at the servant. "I have, haven't I, Hardy?"

"Indeed so, Master Geordie," said the butler.

"Yes, both Wolstan and I were very good, although Wolstan did steal Cook's mutton leg. She was very upset."

"As well she should be," said the baron, eyeing the mastiff with mock sternness. "Now, where is Professor Burry?"

Just as he asked the question, a stout bespectacled gentleman of about sixty years of age, rather red-faced from his exertion, rushed into the hall. "Ramsay, my boy! We did not expect you! By God, it is good to see you." Professor Burry hurried up to the baron and shook his hand enthusiastically. "You must tell us all about London! But you are doubtless tired from your journey. Perhaps you are in need of rest."

"I am fine. Come, let us go to the drawing room." Ramsay, his nephew Geordie, and the professor proceeded to the drawing room, with the dog Wolstan lumbering after them.

From the exterior appearance of the castle, one might have expected the rooms inside to be dark and medieval. However, the baron's drawing room was tastefully decorated in the modern fashion. Indeed, it was not so very different from the drawing rooms of London society. The baron sat down on an elegant sofa and Geordie sat down beside him. Professor Burry lowered himself into a delicate armchair whose classical proportions were ill-suited to his corpulent frame.

Geordie noted that his uncle was carrying some parcels. "What is it you have there, uncle?" he asked curiously.

"Can you not guess, rascal? It is a present for you." The baron handed the largest parcel to the delighted young man.

"Thank you, uncle!" exclaimed Geordie, eagerly tearing the paper wrapping from the gift. "Oh, uncle," he said, gazing at the tin knight upon a horse. He seemed momentarily overwhelmed. "It is splendid!" the boy hugged Ramsay once again. "Oh, thank you!"

"You are easily pleased, nephew," said the baron with a smile. He handed a parcel to the professor. "I know Burry cannot be so easily awed. This is for you, sir."

The professor took the present like an excited child. "There was no need for you to bring me something, my boy."

"Nonsense. Just open it."

Needing no further encouragement, Burry unwrapped the present. "A book! How decent of you, Ramsay." Then, as he picked up the book and examined it, his mouth dropped open in astonishment. "Good Lord! This is a first edition of Donne!" The stout gentlemen sat regarding the book speechlessly.

The baron looked well pleased. "So I have finally dumbfounded you, sir!"

"You have indeed! Ramsay, I cannot accept it. It is too fine a gift."

"You can, sir, and you will," returned the baron with a trace of lordly imperiousness. "There is no one more deserves such a gift."

"You are too generous, my boy."

"Rubbish. Now, tell me what has been happening here

in my absence. I have already heard about the mutton leg.''

Burry laughed. "I daresay that was the most exciting event. Other than that, nothing out of the ordinary has occurred. Geordie's Latin is progressing at a splendid pace. And Mr. Cox is so very pleased with his music lessons. You must hear his Mozart sonata.''

"Indeed, I am most eager to hear it. Go on, Geordie, why don't you play for me?"

The boy put down his knight and went to the piano. He then proceeded to play with remarkable ability for a ten-year-old. At the conclusion of the piece, Ramsay praised his nephew highly, and the delighted Geordie hurried back to his seat on the sofa.

The baron then told of his experience in London and his studies at the British Museum. After some time, Ramsay realized that it was growing late. "I think you had best retire, young man.''

"Oh, Uncle Gervas, can't I stay up longer?"

"I fear not, lad. We shall have plenty of time to talk in the morning.''

"Very well," said Geordie reluctantly. After kissing his uncle good night and bowing politely to the professor, the boy took up his toy knight and departed.

"He's a good lad," said Burry, taking out his pipe.

"Aye, he is," said the baron fondly. Noting that the professor had his pipe in his hand, Ramsay took out another small parcel from his coat. "Oh, I nearly forgot. I brought you some tobacco from that shop in town you always talk about.''

"Bless you, my boy," said Burry, taking the tobacco and filling his pipe. Getting up and going to the fireplace, the professor took up a brand and lit his pipe. Then, returning to his seat, he began to puff contentedly. "Ah, marvelous blend," he said appreciatively. "You must take up a pipe, Ramsay.''

The baron smiled. "I don't think it would suit me. God, it is good to be home.''

Professor Burry eyed the younger man closely. "You cannot mean you did not enjoy yourself even one whit in town."

"That is precisely what I mean. Oh, the work was most enlightening, but I cannot abide London for long."

"I should think a young gentleman like yourself, handsome and titled, would have thoroughly enjoyed himself. There are no more beautiful ladies in the world!"

"Do not spout fustian, sir. I attempted to avoid the ladies."

"Attempted?" The professor looked amused. "That implies that you were not entirely successful." Ramsay frowned, but did not reply. "Come, come, my boy, it appears you have a story to tell. I should like to hear it."

"I was not a rakehell in town, if that is what you think, sir."

Burry laughed. "That is certainly not what I thought. However, I did think you might have met a respectable lady at some social event. I know you planned to see your Digby cousins."

"I could scarcely have avoided it." Ramsay paused and then continued. "I did meet a respectable lady, but I wish I had not met her."

"Ah, the pains of unrequited love," said the professor. "My poor boy."

"Don't be absurd, sir," said the baron. "I did not even like the lady, despite her beauty and reputed charm."

Professor Burry was now very much interested. "Indeed? And who was this lady?"

"Her name is Lady Olivia Dunbar. She is exceedingly beautiful and exceedingly frivolous."

"Did you meet her at the Digbys'?"

Ramsay nodded. "The first time, I did."

"The first time? Then you saw her again?"

"I saw her three times, once at the British Museum and then at a small dinner party at the house of her cousin, Sir Aubrey Roxbury. Roxbury called here last spring. He is the new owner of Fenwyck, and an addlepated fop."

"I recall your speaking of him. But you say you saw this Lady Olivia at the British Museum? Then surely she cannot be so very frivolous."

"She can indeed. It was all some sort of joke. She and her friends had somehow picked me to make sport of."

"Nonsense, my boy."

"No, it is true. I do not know what the game was, but for some reason they feigned interest in me. At first I thought Lady Olivia was a fortune huntress, but then Hedgewod informed me that she is very wealthy. Perhaps he was mistaken."

"Hedgewood. Not Walter Hedgewood?" The baron nodded and Burry shook his head. "How I detested that young man when I had him at Oxford. Although Hedgewood was not much of a thinker, he was the sort to have his facts correct. Don't you think the lady might just have been interested in you?"

The baron regarded Professor Burry as if he were quite bottleheaded. "At dinner she took pains to vex me."

"Then she probably is interested in you!"

Ramsay laughed. "That is nonsensical."

The professor took his pipe from his mouth and pointed it at the baron. "My boy, why do you think it so unbelievable that a lady could be interested in you? You always think the worst. I am sure you misinterpreted Lady Olivia's remarks and she is very disappointed at your lack of gallantry."

"Come, sir," said the baron, "I pray you say nothing more about it. I am weary and think I shall go to bed."

"Of course, Ramsay. You must be exhausted. Good night, my boy." The professor watched the baron leave the room, and when he had gone, Burry frowned and then thoughtfully smoked his pipe. He was very fond of Ramsay, but wished that his young friend were not always so difficult.

The professor had known Ramsay since the baron had been his pupil at Oxford. The young Ramsay had been a quiet, solitary young man, but Burry had been impressed by his keen mind and scholarship. After breaking through the baron's reserve, the professor had found the young man quite likable. Indeed, in time they had developed a very warm relationship, and even after the baron had left university, he continued to correspond with and visit his mentor.

When, two years ago, Ramsay had written to Burry, asking him to tutor his young nephew, the professor had been eager to do so. Having lost his beloved wife less than a year before, Burry had been unhappy at Oxford and was glad of a change. Although his colleagues had been incredulous that he would leave his post to become teacher to a noble brat, Burry never regretted his decision.

Ramsay had been unfailingly kind and generous to him, and Burry had grown very fond of young Geordie. His duties at Hawkesmuir were not onerous, leaving him much time for his own research and writing. He also enjoyed his companionship with the young baron, who was himself a scholar of note. Ramsay was well respected for his writings about medieval history, and the professor had a fatherly pride in his former student's success.

Very much concerned for the baron's welfare, Burry wished that Ramsay might find a wife. Certainly the professor's experience with matrimony had given him a very positive view of the married state. It worried the professor how cynical the baron was about women. Indeed, he many times had told Burry that the ladies were only interested in his title and fortune.

The professor continued to puff on his pipe and gazed thoughtfully into the fire. "Yes, what he needs is a wife," said Burry aloud. But upon further reflection, the professor decided that there was very little he could do to assist the baron with such matters.

8

The heavy traveling coach lumbered along the Northumbrian road through rain and blustery winds. The travelers inside the equipage were exceedingly weary. It was the sixth day of their journey from London, and Olivia, Sophie, and Aubrey were all very eager to reach their destination.

Olivia's usual good spirits were flagging as she looked out the carriage window at the barren moorland. Feeling rather cold, she glanced over at her whippet Mayflower, and seeing the little dog shivering, she wrapped a blanket around her. "Poor Mayflower, you are so cold."

"I am cold too," said Aubrey, "and you do not seem so concerned about me."

Olivia laughed but Sophie did not look at all amused. "Aubrey," she said ill-humoredly, "you deserve to suffer for bringing us here. I think Northumberland is the most dreadful place!"

"Now, now, my dear, you will feel very differently when we arrive at Fenwyck," said Aubrey. "It is just unfortunate that the weather is so bad. But take heart, we are almost there."

"I shall be so glad to get there," said Olivia. "I am so

tired of traveling. Indeed, this is the longest journey I have ever made.''

''That is because Northumberland is at the end of the earth,'' said Sophie.

Olivia laughed again, and Sophie smiled. Seeming now to be in a better humor, Lady Roxbury started to chatter good-naturedly. After less than an hour, Aubrey seemed to recognize the landscape passing by them. ''Why, we are very close indeed. This is Ramsay's property. We should be able to see Hawkesmuir Castle, that is, if the deuced rain and mist will allow it.'' The baronet pointed toward one of the carriage windows. ''Look there, it should be coming into view.''

Very much interested, Olivia peered out. All she could see was moorland and some distant trees. It was so gray and wet and decidedly unpromising-looking. Then, as the road turned, she caught a glimpse of the castle. Set far in the distance and partly hidden by forest, it looked stark and imposing.

''I see it!'' said Sophie. ''Why, it makes me think of Windsor. Just think, Livy, you might have been mistress of it.''

Olivia smiled but made no reply. She was too intent upon the castle. It quickly vanished from view as the coach continued on.

''There is still a chance of it,'' said Sir Aubrey, grinning at his cousin. ''After all, now that we are here, you will have ample opportunity to see the baron.''

''I have no wish to see him,'' replied Olivia, ''and I shall be very vexed with both of you if you persist in speaking about him. Thank heaven, that silly wager is off.''

''Well, I think it is a pity,'' said Sophie. ''It would have been much more amusing to pursue the man. I daresay we will probably be so very bored here.''

''Bored?'' cried Aubrey. ''My dear, it is hunting season!''

''And that is the most boring time of the year,'' said Sophie.

Olivia laughed. "It seems there is a disagreement. I'm sure we will find Northumberland very fascinating, Sophie. It is so very different, after all."

"Indeed it is," said Sophie distastefully.

The baronet prudently tried to divert his wife's attention. "I do think we are nearing the new property. Yes, I think I see the road that leads to Fenwyck."

The ladies peered out the window once again, but could see very little. The carriage turned at the road and made its way along a narrow lane. "There is the house!" exclaimed Sophie.

Olivia caught her first sight of Fenwyck and was favorably impressed by the magnificent country house. Of Georgian design, it was quite modern and it was not at all what Olivia had expected. Indeed, throughout the journey she had imagined an ancient run-down structure, and it was with some relief that she beheld the stately residence.

"It is beautiful, Aubrey," remarked Olivia.

"Yes, it is very nice, my dear," said Sophie.

"The stables are quite exceptional," said Aubrey, pleased at the ladies' response. "I wonder if my hunters have arrived yet."

"Horses!" exclaimed Sophie. "That is all you think about."

"You are unjust, my Sophie." The baronet paused and smiled at her. "I think about hounds as well."

The ladies burst into laughter, and as the carriage pulled to a halt, they were all in much better humors. A rough-looking servant hurried out into the rain to open the carriage door, and soon Aubrey, the ladies, and Mayflower were inside the house. They were met in the entry hall by a somberly dressed matronly woman.

"Mrs. Colfax, how glad we are to be finally here."

The woman eyed the ladies curiously and curtsied.

"Ladies, I must present the housekeeper, Mrs. Colfax. Mrs. Colfax, this is Lady Roxbury and my cousin Lady Olivia Dunbar."

The housekeeper curtsied again. "Honored to meet you, ladies," she said in a north-country accent.

"Mrs. Colfax was housekeeper to the Wendells, the previous owners of the house."

"Aye, that I was," said the servant. "I have been with the house since the day it was built. Nigh on thirty years."

"How very admirable, I'm sure," said Aubrey. "Now we are all very weary, Mrs. Colfax. We shall go to our rooms. I do hope dinner will be ready at seven."

"Aye, sir, it will be ready. Now I shall be very happy to escort you, sir and ladies," said the housekeeper, and they followed her out of the entry hall.

Olivia found her rooms at Fenwyck spacious but very Spartanly furnished. Her bedchamber was also very cold, since the fire had not been made in her fireplace. A short time later a servant appeared and lit the fire, and when he had gone, Olivia and Mayflower hurried over to it to warm themselves. After standing there for some time, Olivia walked to the window and looked out. The rain was still coming down, and although it was afternoon, it was very dark and gloomy. A slight smile came to her face as she peered out into the sodden grounds. Even though Fenwyck did not thus far seem a very promising place, it was far better than Wessex. At least she was away from Jocasta and her relations.

There was a knock on her door and she turned to see Sophie enter. Lady Roxbury looked around Olivia's room and frowned disapprovingly. "I see your room is even worse than ours. Why, there is hardly a stick of furniture in it. And I have seen the drawing room! My dear, it is almost empty. I am so irked with Aubrey. He is so concerned with his precious hunters that he does not seem to care at all about the lack of comforts in this house."

"Sophie, you must simply buy some more furniture."

"I daresay purchasing furniture is not so simple in such a place as this. And it is so tiresome that our maids are not here yet. I don't know how I shall survive without my

Clara. I do wish they had come with us instead of traveling separately with the other servants and luggage.''

"They will be here tomorrow.''

Sophie nodded. "But what shall I do tonight? We must dress for dinner.''

Olivia laughed. "I daresay we will both manage somehow.''

Noting that the whippet was now curled up by the fire, Sophie smiled. "At least Mayflower seems happy to be here.''

"It won't be so bad,'' replied Olivia. "You will see. I would not be surprised to find that soon we will enjoy it better than anyplace.''

"Well, that would surprise me very much.'' Sophie smiled. "At least we are done with traveling and those dreadful coaching inns. Would you prefer to rest awhile longer, Livy, or would you like to see the house? Mrs. Colfax is most eager to show it to us.''

"Oh, I have rested enough and would very much like to have the tour.'' The two ladies left the room together, and Mayflower scurried after them.

Olivia stared at the blank sheet of paper before her. She was finding the task of writing a letter to Edward and Jocasta very difficult. It had been two days since they had arrived at Fenwyck, and the visit was getting off to a most unpromising start.

The weather had continued to be abominable, cold and rainy. The incessant rain had confined them to the house, and the usually fun-loving threesome was beginning to become disheartened. It was not easy for Olivia to write a cheerful letter, but she resolved to do so. She did not want her brother and sister-in-law to think she was not enjoying herself. Dipping her quill pen into the ink, Olivia began an optimistic account of their journey and the countryside around Fenwyck.

Nearly an hour later, Olivia completed the letter, and

just as she was beginning to reread it, Sophie burst into her sitting room. "Olivia," she cried, "we have a visitor!"

The whippet Mayflower, who had been lying dejectedly at her mistress's feet, rose and wagged her tail at Lady Roxbury. Olivia smiled at her friend. "How extraordinary! A visitor at Fenwyck! Whoever could it be?"

"I am sorry to report that it is not Lord Ramsay," replied Sophie mischievously. "It is Mr. Malvern."

Remembering the baron's negative reaction to the mention of that gentleman's name, Olivia found herself most curious to make his acquaintance. "I should like to meet him."

"Then let us hurry down and do so," said Sophie eagerly. After commanding a disappointed Mayflower to stay there, Olivia followed Sophie out of the room.

When they arrived at the drawing room, Olivia and Sophie found Aubrey and their visitor in animated conversation. The gentlemen rose quickly as the ladies entered, and Olivia had opportunity to study the caller.

She was struck by Malvern's great size. He was tall and massive, and Olivia decided she had never seen a man who could match him in breadth of shoulders. He was handsome in a rough sort of way, with a broad square-jawed face with regular features. He had no pretensions to dandyism and was dressed simply in the manner of a country sporting gentleman. Yet his coat was of excellent cut, fitting his wide frame admirably, and the nankeen pantaloons that covered his well-muscled legs were fashionable although mud-spattered.

"Ladies, you must meet the squire. I know he is eager to meet you. May I present Mr. Roger Malvern? Squire, this is Lady Roxbury and my cousin Lady Olivia Dunbar."

· Malvern smiled first at Sophie and then directed a bold look at Olivia. He bowed. "Your servant, ladies. What good fortune to welcome such lovely ladies as yourselves. I daresay all the females in the county will be overcome with jealousy at the sight of you."

Sophie acknowledged the compliment with a delighted laugh. "I see that Northumbrian gentlemen are well versed in flummery, sir."

"It is not flummery, I assure you," said Malvern, looking again at Olivia.

Olivia was finding the gentleman's scrutiny a trifle unsettling. "How nice it is to receive a visitor, Mr. Malvern," she said. "You are our first caller."

"I consider that an honor," replied the squire.

"Come," said Aubrey, "let us all sit down."

Olivia sat down on the sofa and noted that Malvern seemed quick to assume the place next to her. Sophie, too, did not fail to notice this, and decided that her friend had made yet another conquest. "We were just talking about hunting," continued Aubrey.

"Oh dear!" cried Sophie in mock dismay. "I might have known!"

Malvern grinned. "I know that ladies do not find the subject as fascinating as gentlemen."

"Indeed," said Aubrey. "I fear my wife thinks hunting rather a bore. But my cousin Livy does not. She is quite the sportswoman. Why, she hunts and rides as hard as any man."

Malvern eyed Olivia appreciatively. "Then your beauty is not the only remarkable thing about you, Lady Olivia. I shall now be even more eager for the hunt."

Olivia could not fail to compare Malvern's reaction to her hunting with that of Baron Ramsay. She remembered that baron had frowned so disapprovingly at her, while Malvern appeared quite delighted.

"Livy is not one of those females who attempt to hunt and just get in the way," said Aubrey.

"I am glad of it," said Malvern. "Till now the only woman fit to share the field at our hunts was my sister. Caroline rides like a demon. Why, once she rode a horse to death," said the squire proudly.

Olivia tried to hide her appalled reaction to this remark.

"The devil!" cried Aubrey. "I hope we will have the pleasure of meeting her."

"You will. She lives not far from here. She is married to Sir Clarence Horsley, but why she married him is a mystery to me. He is the most hen-hearted fellow, and is so fat he can scarcely sit a horse. Thank God, Caroline is man enough for both of them."

"You seem very hard on your brother-in-law, Mr. Malvern," said Olivia, regarding him with disapproval.

Malvern laughed. "Once you meet him, ma'am, you'll think I have been kind."

Both Aubrey and Sophie laughed at this exhibition of wit, but Olivia was beginning to take a dislike to the gentleman.

"Well, I do hope you will tell your sister to call upon us, sir," said Sophie. "I do wish to meet all of local society. Why, thus far, we have met only you and Baron Ramsay."

"Ramsay?" said the squire, regarding her in astonishment. "You cannot mean that he has called on you?"

"Oh, no," said Sophie, "we met him in town."

"You met him in London?" Malvern's expression indicated that he found this information quite remarkable.

"We met the baron at Lady Digby's party," said Sophie.

"I did not think him the sort to attend parties," said Malvern. "By God, he is an odd fellow."

"Odd?" said Olivia, resenting Malvern's contemptuous tone. She adopted a puzzled expression. "I did not think him at all odd. Why, we all thought his lordship very charming. When he dined with us, he was the most amusing gentleman."

The squire was so amazed at this remark that he did not notice the look the Roxburys were exchanging. "You had him to dinner?"

Sophie, amused by her friend's words, was eager to join Olivia in quizzing their guest. "It was an intimate little gathering. How we enjoyed the baron's conversation. Indeed, I think Olivia developed a *tendre* for him.''

"Sophie!" exclaimed Olivia in mock horror. "Do not reveal my secrets!"

Malvern frowned. "You ladies must be speaking of a different gentleman than the one I know."

"Perhaps so," said Olivia. "We speak of Baron Ramsay of Hawkesmuir. He is a most distinguished gentleman and a scholar as well."

"He is that," said Malvern scornfully. "He is as bookish as a schoolmaster. I never thought books the proper occupation for a gentleman."

"And what is the proper occupation for a gentleman?" asked Olivia.

"Hunting, of course," returned the squire. "And Ramsay does not hunt."

"That is peculiar," said Aubrey. "Ramsay did appear to have an antipathy toward hunting."

"He hasn't the belly for it," said Malvern. "How different he is from old Ramsay. Aye, his father rode with the Malvern and there was never a more fearless horseman. I know he was ashamed of his son, who preferred a book and a warm fire to a go at a fox on a chill morning. I have known Ramsay since we were boys. He was a puling little runt with only his family and fortune to recommend him. His bad leg made him pitiable. I do not think he is very much different now."

Although Olivia certainly had no love for Ramsay, she hurried to his defense. "You do Lord Ramsay an injustice, sir. I think him an admirable gentleman."

Malvern frowned at Olivia, but said nothing further about the baron. Aubrey returned the conversation to hunting and Malvern discoursed long on the merits of his pack of hounds, which, according to that gentleman, was the best in all of the north country. After finally exhausting this topic, the squire departed.

When he was gone, Olivia laughed. "Good heavens,

what an unlikable fellow. I must say that after meeting Lord Ramsay and now Mr. Malvern, it seems that Northumbrian gentlemen are very unpromising indeed.''

Sophie laughed in return. '''What do you mean? From your words just now, I thought you were quite enamored of Ramsay. Certainly Mr. Malvern thought so.''

''Indeed,'' said Aubrey, regarding his cousin with some irritation, ''why did you feel it necessary to gammon our guest?''

''Oh, Aubrey, I found him insufferable,'' said Olivia. ''You cannot mean you like him?''

''I do. He is really a good fellow.''

''And he is rather handsome,'' added Sophie, ''and he does have the finest pack of hounds in the north country.''

The ladies laughed and Sir Aubrey frowned. ''Having a fine pack of hounds is no small matter. And Malvern is not merely boasting.''

''But I am not criticizing his hounds, Aubrey,'' said Olivia. ''I just thought it abominable how he spoke of Lord Ramsay.''

''A man whom I thought you detested,'' said the baronet.

''It does not signify what I think of Lord Ramsay. I thought it very ungentlemanly of Malvern to disparage him so.''

''I agree,'' said Sophie.

Aubrey said nothing further in defense of his new friend, but it was clear from his expression that he was irked with the ladies' remarks.

9

Later that afternoon Olivia began to grow restless. The weather had cleared, and although it was still chilly, Olivia was eager to get out of the house. Her suggestion to Sophie that they go for a walk was met with little enthusiasm by Lady Roxbury, who thought it too wet and muddy. Sir Aubrey, intent upon the pages of *The Sporting Magazine*, agreed with his wife.

Undaunted, Olivia announced that she would go out with Mayflower. After changing into a plum-colored walking dress and informing her delighted whippet that they were going for a walk, Olivia started out. She was stopped at the door by the baronet, who cautioned her not to go very far. Assuring Aubrey that she would go just a short distance, Olivia and the dog set off.

The brisk air felt wonderful to her after being confined inside, and she walked quickly away from the house. Mayflower, ecstatic at being out with her mistress, raced ahead. Olivia smiled at the dog and then looked about her. Although decidedly unimpressed with the scenery around Fenwyck upon her arrival, Olivia now viewed the landscape more favorably. The barren moorland had a wild charm and the hills beyond it were unquestionably lovely.

Following a winding path, Olivia had soon walked some distance. She appreciated the quiet and unaccustomed solitude, which allowed her much time for reflection. She was suddenly glad to be there in Northumberland and away from the bustle of town and her problems with her sister-in-law. Olivia smiled as she thought of Edward now in Wessex with Jocasta's family. "Poor Edward," she said aloud, remembering that her brother was not at all fond of his mother-in-law and was quite intimidated by his father-in-law, the duke. How lucky that she had escaped with the Roxburys, thought Olivia. Her only regret was being parted so long from her nephews and niece. Indeed, Olivia was quite devoted to her brother's children and missed them already.

Mayflower caught sight of a rabbit and, her coursing blood coming to fore, dashed after it. The swift little hound could run great distances, and Olivia was tempted to call her back. However, knowing that the whippet was in need of a run, Olivia allowed her to continue her pursuit of her prey. When the dog rejoined her mistress a short time later, Mayflower seemed disappointed at her failure to catch the rabbit. Olivia laughed. "My poor Mayflower, do not be disheartened. There are many more rabbits about." The dog wagged her tail and ran ahead.

Olivia was enjoying her walk so much that she did not seem to note how much time was passing and how far from Fenwyck she had gone. While in the country, she was accustomed to walking many miles, distances that tired most other young ladies. She continued on for some time, reluctant to return to the house. However, the position of the sun in the gray sky made her finally realize she must turn back. Olivia stopped and sighed, wishing she could go on. The weather was so perfect for walking, and she was having such a lovely time. However, Olivia knew that if she wished to get back before dark, she must hurry. "Well, Mayflower, I fear we must return to Fenwyck.

Aubrey will be sorely vexed with me for being gone so long. Come along, my girl.''

The whippet came obediently toward her, but just as Olivia turned to start back, a rabbit appeared from the undergrowth and Mayflower rushed excitedly after it. Olivia called to the hound, but the dog seemed too intent upon the chase to heed her mistress. Irritated at the whippet's unusual disobedience, Olivia stopped and watched Mayflower vanish into the darkening moor.

After waiting for a time, and continuing to call the dog's name, Olivia began to wonder what had become of her. Worried at the dog's continued absence, Olivia left the path and started in the direction Mayflower had taken.

Hurrying across the uneven terrain, Olivia suddenly tripped and fell. She shouted a most unladylike epithet as she landed hard on the ground. Thinking uncharitable thoughts about her beloved whippet, Olivia started to get up, but as she put her weight on one foot, pain from her ankle made her wince. ''Oh, no,'' she said aloud, the horrible thought of being unable to walk coming to her. Her fears were confirmed when she tried once again to rise and experienced another sharp pain.

Olivia sat back down on the ground and was very much aware of the gravity of the situation. The light was quickly fading and a mist was rising from the lonely moorland. She had no idea how far she was from Fenwyck, but knew the manor house had disappeared from view some time ago. She might be three or four miles from it, and she had passed no other habitation along the path.

Mayflower appeared beside her, and although blaming the dog for the disaster, Olivia was comforted by the whippet's presence. ''Mayflower, you are a very naughty dog. You have got your mistress in a fine pickle.'' The hound looked suitably chastened and licked her mistress's face. ''It is not so easy to make amends, my girl,'' she

said, stroking the dog. "I don't know what we will do."
Olivia felt her ankle tentatively. Perhaps if she rested it a
bit, she would be able to walk. However, she thought it
very unlikely that she could get back to Fenwyck.

It was cold and the ground damp, and Olivia shivered
and pulled her cloak more tightly about her. Perhaps a
farmer might come by, she reasoned, and although thinking this a remote possibility, Olivia called out for help.
Mayflower barked as well, but it was soon apparent that
there was no one within hearing.

After a time, Olivia tried to stand up again. She succeeded in getting to her feet after much effort, but the pain
was unbearable. Fighting back tears, Olivia sat down once
again. She hugged Mayflower. "What are we to do?" she
said. Olivia tried to take heart from the knowledge that
Aubrey would soon come looking for her, but since the
baronet did not know which way she had gone, it might be
some time before he found her. The mist and increasing
darkness were now making it almost impossible to see,
and Olivia valiantly attempted to suppress her fears.

Suddenly the whippet's ears pricked up and her nose
twitched inquisitively. "Do you hear something, Mayflower?" asked Olivia, straining her ears, but hearing
nothing. The little dog then ran off, leaving her mistress
perplexed and uneasy.

She then heard the dog barking and the unmistakable
snorting of a horse. Olivia cried out once again. "Is
someone there? Help! Help me, please!" At the sound of
hoofbeats and Mayflower's continued barking, Olivia experienced a tremendous sense of relief. "I am here!" she
shouted.

However, she caught her breath as an enormous black
horse appeared out of the mist. Olivia suddenly remembered tales from her childhood of ghostly creatures roam-
ing the deserted countryside. Mounted on the spectral
steed was a rider who appeared a shadowy and faceless

figure. Mayflower eagerly rushing up to her gave her courage to speak. "I need your help, sir. I am injured."

The rider directed his horse toward Olivia and soon reached her. He dismounted and, kneeling beside her, asked solicitously, "Are you badly hurt?"

Glimpsing his face in the darkness, Olivia looked surprised. "Lord Ramsay!"

The baron regarded her with a startled expression. "Lady Olivia?"

"Yes, it is I. I fear I have made a muddle of things. I have been out walking from Fenwyck."

"Good God! That is more than five miles away."

"Oh dear, I did not know I had come so far. I lost track of time. Sir Aubrey and Lady Roxbury will be so upset with me."

"As well they should," returned the baron. "One does not roam about these moors in the dark."

"I assure you, my lord," said Olivia defensively, "it was not my intention to be here in the dark. We were going back and Mayflower saw a rabbit and ran off. She would not come when I called and I went after her. But I fell and was so worried I would be here all night. I thank Providence that you have come to rescue me."

"You must thank your whippet for that. Had she not run after me I would not have known you were here."

Olivia scratched the dog behind the ears affectionately. "Mayflower, you have redeemed yourself."

"Do you think your ankle is broken, Lady Olivia?" said the baron in a businesslike manner.

She shrugged. "I do not know."

"Let me see it. Which one is hurt?"

"The right one, but . . ." began Olivia, but before she could protest his examining her ankle, Ramsay picked up her foot. She grimaced.

"It is very painful?" Olivia nodded. "It appears swollen," continued the baron. "Your boot must come off. I fear I shall have to cut it."

'Very well,'' she said lightly. ''They were not quite the thing anyway.''

The baron smiled slightly, and taking a knife from his boot top, he neatly sliced the leather and removed the boot. ''That is better,'' said Olivia.

After further examination of her ankle, Ramsay looked over at her. ''I do not think it's broken, but I shall fetch Dr. Penney to confirm it. I shall have to get you to Hawkesmuir.''

''Hawkesmuir?'' replied Olivia. ''But I must get back to Fenwyck. Aubrey and Sophie must be so worried.''

''I fear, ma'am, that would be unwise. Hawkesmuir is only a short ride from here. I shall send a message to the Roxburys that you are there.''

Realizing the sense of his words, Olivia nodded. Without further comment, Ramsay picked Olivia up with surprising ease and, carrying her to the horse, he placed her atop the tall stallion. He them climbed agilely up behind her. As the baron urged his horse ahead, Olivia smiled. How odd it was to find herself on a horse with Ramsay, his arms around her. Surely that gentleman must be cursing the fates that had once more brought them together.

In truth, the baron was thinking nothing of the kind. Since he had last seen her, Ramsay had thought of Olivia often. Although she had infuriated and confounded him, the baron had not been as immune to the lady's charms as she had thought. At that moment he found her proximity rather unsettling, but not at all unpleasant.

''I am sorry to so trouble you, Lord Ramsay,'' said Olivia. ''You must think me a great goose.'' When the baron remained silent, Olivia laughed. ''It would be kind if you would deny it, even though you believe it to be true.''

Ramsay smiled. ''Then I shall endeavor to oblige you. You are not a great goose, Lady Olivia.''

''You are kind, my lord. I'll warrant you are surprised to find me here.''

"I admit I did not expect to find a lone female on the moors."

"I meant, to find me here in Northumberland."

"I must confess I was somewhat surprised, ma'am, but then, as I recall, you did intend to accompany the Roxburys to meet the marriageable Mr. Malvern."

Olivia smiled. "Yes, and as good fortune would have it, I met him just today." She turned and smiled impishly at him. To her satisfaction, the baron was frowning.

"I hope he was everything you expected," said Ramsay coolly.

"Oh, yes, and he was so handsome, too." Thoroughly enjoying herself, Olivia would have continued quizzing the baron, but the sight of Hawkesmuir Castle looming ahead took her mind from the squire. The enormous fortress appeared a most uninviting place in the dim light. "Do you live here alone, my lord?"

The baron denoted a touch of apprehension in her voice and he smiled. "Yes, but for a few companionable ghouls."

Olivia laughed and he joined her. "You do have a sense of humor, Lord Ramsay," she said.

They arrived at the castle gate and Ramsay shouted for a servant. His summons was immediately heeded by a burly youth who eyed Olivia with unabashed astonishment. "M'lord?"

Olivia suppressed a smile, thinking that the baron had called the servant to carry her inside. However, Ramsay got off his horse and lifted her down himself. Holding Olivia in his arms, he addressed the servant. "Take Destre, Jem."

The young man continued to gape at Olivia, but then, noting his master's stern look, he nodded and led the big horse away. Ramsay started to the door with her, Mayflower close at his heels. "Really, my lord," said Olivia, "I think I could walk with assistance."

"You'll not walk until Dr. Penney has a look at you."

As they approached the door, it was opened and the baron's butler regarded them in surprise. "The lady is injured, Hardy," said his lordship. "Tell Crowley to fetch Dr. Penney. And have Mrs. Hamilton ready a room from her ladyship."

"Aye, m'lord," said the servant, hurrying off.

Olivia glanced around the entry hall and was glad to find it not so forbidding. Ramsay carried her from the hall into the drawing room. Seated in the room were an elderly man and a young boy, both of whom looked up as they entered. Their startled expressions nearly caused Olivia to burst into laughter. The baron said nothing as he walked past them and deposited her on a sofa near the fireplace. Mayflower hurried after them, but stopped short at sight of an enormous mastiff stretched out in front of the fire. The big dog regarded the whippet curiously and then wagged his tail. Mayflower needed no further encouragement and scampered over to the mastiff.

"Ramsay, my boy," said Professor Burry, who was still amazed at the sight of the baron carrying a lovely maiden into his drawing room, "what has happened?" Both Burry and Geordie hurried over to Olivia and the baron.

"Are you injured, ma'am?" asked the boy, regarding Olivia with wide dark eyes.

"Oh, it is nothing serious. I fell when walking. I twisted my ankle." Olivia smiled her famous smile at them. "It was so lucky that Lord Ramsay happened by. I might still be out on the moors but for him."

"I have sent for Dr. Penney," said the baron. Then, noting that Burry and Geordie were looking expectantly at him, Ramsay made the introduction. "Lady Olivia, may I present Professor Burry and my nephew Geordie Sinclair. Gentlemen, this is Lady Olivia Dunbar."

The professor appeared further astonished at hearing the

lady's name and regarded his young friend curiously. "Your servant, ma'am," said Burry, bowing gallantly to the lady.

Geordie was quick to follow the professor's example. He smiled at her and bowed politely. "How do you do, ma'am?"

"How do you do, Master George?" returned Olivia, regarding the boy with interest. She could not fail to note a resemblance between Geordie and his uncle. The boy had Ramsay's dark hair and eyes, but his bright smile was very different from the dour expression that was usually on the baron's countenance.

"Oh, do call me Geordie, ma'am," said the youngster. "No one calls me George except Uncle when he is angry."

Olivia smiled at the baron. "And is that very often, Geordie?"

The boy grinned mischievously. "Oh, no, my lady, for I am usually very good."

Olivia laughed. "I am glad to hear it, young man."

Geordie appeared quite taken with the visitor. "Could I get you something, Lady Olivia? Are you hungry?"

"You are kind, sir," said Olivia, smiling at the lad. "I am not very hungry at present."

"Perhaps you might ask Mrs. Hamilton to get a blanket for the lady, Geordie," suggested the baron. Eager to be of service, Geordie hurried off.

"What a charming little boy," said Olivia. "He is so like my nephews. But truly, Lord Ramsay, there is no need to trouble yourself on my behalf. I am fine."

"We will allow Dr. Penney to decide that, ma'am," said Ramsay. "He should be here soon. After we have his report, I shall send word to Fenwyck."

Olivia nodded and thanked him.

"You are staying at Fenwyck?" said Burry, seating himself in a chair near Olivia.

"Yes, my cousin Sir Aubrey Roxbury has taken the property. He, Lady Roxbury, and I arrived just two days ago from town."

"How good it is to meet you, Lady Olivia," replied the professor. "His lordship told me of meeting you in London."

Olivia glanced over at Ramsay with an amused look. "Did he?"

The baron looked embarrassed and cast a disapproving look at Burry, who ignored it and continued. "I see Ramsay was right about your being a beauty."

Although dearly loving the professor, the baron could have cheerfully strangled his mentor at that moment. Fortunately, there was a diversion as Geordie rushed back into the room with a blanket. He hurried to Olivia and solicitously placed it around her. The boy happily received Olivia's grateful thanks and then noticed Mayflower for the first time. "It is a whippet! What a fine dog. And already she and Wolstan are such great friends."

The mastiff did look very happy with his new companion, and when the small hound came over to Geordie, the big dog followed. "Oh, you are a handsome fellow," said Olivia, addressing the mastiff. The huge animal came over to her and put his heavily jowled face in her lap.

"Mind your manners, brute," warned the baron.

Olivia laughed and gently stroked the dog's wrinkled brow. "But he is being a complete darling, my lord." Mayflower, unhappy at the attention her mistress was giving Wolstan, left Geordie and hurried to Olivia, who patted her obligingly.

"I see you are very fond of dogs," said Burry. "You share that with Ramsay, ma'am." Again the baron eyed the older man disapprovingly and again Burry took no note of him. "Yes, how fortunate that you are to be our neighbor, Lady Olivia. Is it not fortunate, Ramsay?"

Olivia looked expectantly at the baron. "Yes, it is," replied Ramsay gruffly. "I wonder how long Penney will be in getting here. The village is not very far."

Happily, the physician arrived a short time later. Dr.

Penney was a thin sober-faced man of middle years. A gentleman of few words, the doctor wasted no time in exchanging pleasantries with his patient, but immediately examined Olivia's ankle with expert care.

"Well, Penney?" said the baron a trifle impatiently.

"There are no broken bones, my lord," he said. "However, it is a bad sprain and the lady must take care to allow it time to heal. You must stay off your feet, madam."

"Then you must continue to carry her, uncle," said Geordie, and the surgeon directed an inquiring gaze at his lordship.

"That will be all then, Penney," said the baron brusquely. "Thank you and good evening." The doctor nodded and took his leave. Ramsay turned to Olivia. "Then I shall send word to the Roxburys that you are staying here."

Geordie seemed elated. "I am sure that you will have to stay at least a fornight, Lady Olivia."

Olivia laughed. "I pray you do not distress your uncle, Geordie."

Geordie looked over at his uncle in surprise. "But could not Lady Olivia stay a fortnight, Uncle Gervas?"

"The lady is welcome to stay as long as she wants," returned the baron.

"Then you must stay until you are better, Lady Olivia," said the boy.

"I fear, Geordie," said Olivia with a smile, "that I should never impose on his lordship's hospitality to such an extent. And besides, I am a guest at Fenwyck and must soon go back."

Geordie looked disappointed but then brightened. "At least you will be here for dinner and then tomorrow. It will be great fun."

"Geordie," said Ramsay, "I think we had best allow Lady Olivia to rest until dinner." He looked over at her. "Your room has been prepared, ma'am. I shall take you there now."

"I'm certain that I could walk with assistance, Lord Ramsay. I need not be carried like an infant."

"Oh, nonsense," said Professor Burry. "It is no trouble for a strong young man like his lordship to carry a little thing like yourself."

The baron fixed an exasperated look at the professor and then wordlessly went to the couch and picked Olivia up once again. "Do take care of your back, my lord," she said. Olivia tried not to laugh at his expression as he started out of the room.

10

Olivia awakened at the sound of the maid entering the room. The whippet, who had been curled up at the foot of the bed, lifted her head to regard the servant inquisitively. "Your pardon, m'lady," said the maid, bobbing a curtsy. "I am sorry to disturb you."

Olivia sat up. "That is quite all right."

"Mr. Crowley be returned from Fenwyck, m'lady, and he has brought you a letter as well as some clothes." The maid extended a salver to Olivia.

"Thank you," said Olivia, taking the letter and looking at the maid. "I cannot imagine how the man returned from Fenwyck so quickly."

The maid smiled. "There has been ample time for that, m'lady. 'Tis past seven."

"Past seven? Oh dear, I have slept almost two hours?"

The other woman nodded. "I think your ladyship was in need of it."

Olivia smiled and opened the letter. She read the note that was written in Sophie's highly ornamented hand. "Dearest Livy," it began. "Aubrey and I were mad with worry about you. We were relieved, but also very surprised, to find you were at Hawkesmuir. I am so glad that your injury was not severe, and that Lord Ramsay has promised to take such good care of you. I have sent over some clothes and we will expect you back at Fenwyck tomorrow. Do not vex Lord Ramsay overmuch. Your devoted Sophie." Olivia smiled at her friend's last sentence and put the letter aside.

"Do you wish to go to dinner, m'lady?" asked the maid.

"Oh yes, I should like that very much, but I hope his lordship doesn't think he has to carry me about."

"Oh, we have found her late ladyship's bath chair and, but for the stairs, there is no need for your ladyship to be carried about."

Olivia found herself strangely disappointed at this, but smiled. "That is good. I do hate to trouble the baron so. He has been very kind."

"Oh, that be his way, m'lady," replied the maid matter-of-factly. "He be the kindest gentleman."

Olivia was rather surprised at the servant's praise of the baron, for she would have judged him to be a stern and demanding master. "Professor Burry also appears to be a kind gentleman," said Olivia, "and young Master Geordie is such a sweet boy."

"Aye," said the servant, "the professor be liked by all here, and wee Geordie be everyone's darling. What a dear lad! What a tragedy that he was left an orphan at such an early age."

"I am sorry to hear that," said Olivia. "Has he lived at Hawkesmuir long?"

"Aye, m'lady, since he was only two. His mother was his lordship's only sister and she died of fever just before the lad's second birthday. His father, Captain Sinclair, died two months before Geordie was born. The poor lad has no one but his lordship, who has been more father than uncle to him."

"You mean the baron has raised the boy himself?"

"Aye, m'lady. And he was only a lad of nineteen

himself when Master Geordie came to us! He was go good with the boy. 'Tis a pity he has no children of his own.''

Olivia tried to imagine the baron with the infant Geordie on his knee, but had a difficult time doing so. Ramsay seemed such a cool, reserved man, she thought.

"Is Professor Burry related to Lord Ramsay?'' asked Olivia.

"Nay, m'lady. Mr. Burry be young Master Geordie's tutor.''

Olivia regarded the maid curiously. It appeared she had misjudged the baron. Indeed, she had taken him for a proud, arrogant man and would not have thought him the sort who would have a tutor as an intimate acquaintance. Although tutors and governesses were not precisely servants, they were scarcely treated as equals by their employers. Yet Ramsay was obviously fond of and even deferential to the professor.

"If it be agreeable to your ladyship, I shall fetch Annie to assist me and we will help you to the dressing room,'' said the maid.

"Yes, that is fine,'' replied Olivia, and as the servant left the room, she continued to reflect upon the baron.

Professor Burry sat in the drawing room smoking his pipe. He looked up as Ramsay entered the room. To the professor's satisfaction, he noted that the baron had taken special care with his appearance. "Are those new evening clothes, Ramsay?''

The baron seemed uncomfortable under the professor's scrutiny, but he tried to appear nonchalant. "I did buy some clothes in town.''

Burry raised an eyebrow. "Well, you look dashed handsome, lad. That coat appears to be the hand of a master. The renowned Weston?''

Ramsay reddened. "Yes, Weston.''

The professor grinned. "Your lady will think you dashing.''

The baron frowned. "I pray you cease this ridiculous talk, sir. Lady Olivia is scarcely 'my' lady."

"My dear boy, she obviously has her cap set for you. Why else would she have pursued you all the way from London? You are a deuced lucky fellow, Ramsay, and she is deuced lucky too."

The baron directed a pained look at the professor, but had no opportunity to reply as a maid entered the room. "Her ladyship be ready to come down to dinner, m'lord."

Ramsay nodded to the maid and, glancing one more time at Professor Burry, he followed the servant from the room. Nearing the great stone stairway, Ramsay stopped as he looked up and caught sight of Olivia leaning on the arm of another maid. He could not help but be struck by her beauty. She wore a gown of blue silk covered with lace and her lovely blond tresses were elegantly coiffed in the French style. She smiled down at him and he experienced a most disquieting sensation.

Olivia looked down and was surprised at the baron's appearance. His excellently cut coat of black superfine fitted his trim form to perfection and his wild black hair had been arranged with evident care. Olivia thought he looked very handsome. "Lord Ramsay," she called to him, "just stay where you are and I shall slide down the banister to you."

He smiled and started up the stairs. "I daresay it will be safer for me to carry you down."

"I scarcely think it would be safer, my lord," replied Olivia.

The baron arrived at the top of the stairs. "I assure you, I shall not drop you. You need not fear for your safety." He picked her up and Olivia placed her arms around his neck.

"It is not my safety that concerns me, sir," said Olivia with a mischievous look. "I was thinking again of your back."

He smiled again and started down the stairs. They were

met at the bottom by Geordie with the wheeled chair. "I shall push you, Lady Olivia," said the boy as his uncle placed her in the chair.

"How kind of you, sir," said Olivia. "Indeed, Geordie, you are so very chivalrous."

"But it is Uncle Gervas who is chivalrous," replied the boy. "It is his specialty."

Olivia regarded the baron with amusement. "What an intriguing man you are, Lord Ramsay. No wonder you rescued me. I was a damsel in need of a chivalrous knight."

"Geordie was referring to my study of the medieval code of chivalry. As you are undoubtedly aware, Lady Olivia, the code was embodied in the noble Baron de Courcy."

Olivia burst into laughter. "It was very bad of me to feign knowledge of the book, but I could not let you think me completely birdwitted. I now confess I know nothing of such things and I pray you do not ask me to translate any Norman French."

Geordie entered the conversation. "Oh, Uncle will not ask you to do that, Lady Olivia. He knows Norman French. And Latin, and Greek, and German, and—"

"That is enough, Geordie," said the baron hastily. "I am sure Lady Olivia is not interested in these matters."

"But I am, my lord," said Olivia. "I suppose you also know Hebrew, Arabic, and Hindi?"

Ramsay smiled. "I must admit my Hindi is not very fluent."

Olivia laughed again and Geordie started to wheel her toward the dining room. Burry met them in the hall. "Lady Olivia, you are a picture of loveliness. I do hope your ankle is not troubling you."

"Oh, it is much improved, but everyone still insists on treating me like an invalid. I do wish you all would quit fussing over me."

"Do not deprive us of the pleasure," said the professor with a courtly bow.

"I see that Baron Ramsay is not the only gentleman well versed in chivalry in this house," said Olivia.

"Indeed not," said Burry, smiling over at Ramsay. "It was I who first interested him in the subject when he was a lad of sixteen at Oxford."

"Oh, you are a professor at Oxford, sir?" asked Olivia.

"He was one of the best," interjected the baron. "Indeed, I realize I was very selfish in having the professor come here to tutor my nephew." Olivia could not help but note the obvious affection between the two men and she was rather touched.

They entered the dining room and Ramsay assisted Olivia from the bath chair to a seat at the table. The castle dining room had retained a very medieval appearance, and having been talking of knights and chivalry, Olivia imagined the vast dining hall as it might have been during the days of King Richard the Lion Hearted. However, the first course laid before them was not at all medieval. Indeed, she thought with a smile, it was as good as the food at the Halliburton Arms.

"And so, Lady Olivia," said Burry, "are you enjoying your stay at Fenwyck?"

"We have only just arrived, but my visit here in certainly most enjoyable."

"I don't imagine you have yet had opportunity to meet any of the ladies and gentlemen hereabouts?" said the professor.

"Lady Olivia has met Squire Malvern," said the baron.

"He is a terrible man," said Geordie. "I hope you did not like him."

"Geordie," said the baron sternly. "It is rude to speak so, and Lady Olivia may like whom she pleases. Malvern is a popular man in some circles."

Geordie looked rather chastened. "Well, I do not like him."

"Neither do I," said Olivia. When Ramsay regarded her in surprise, she laughed. "Geordie, I was bamming your uncle earlier, acting as though I found Mr. Malvern charming. I daresay, I doubt if even his hounds find him charming.'' Geordie laughed delightedly and a slight smile appeared on the baron's face. ''I know it is not right to speak ill of someone,'' continued Olivia, ''but Mr. Malvern is such an unpleasant man.''

Burry nodded. ''The man is hunting mad. He thinks there is nothing more to life than to dash after a pack of howling hounds.''

''Professor Burry,'' said the baron, trying to stop the older man from saying anything more derogatory about the sport, ''I believe Lady Olivia hunts.''

Professor Burry looked as though he had committed a gaffe, but Olivia hastened to reassure him. ''But I am not hunting mad. Unfortunately, my cousin Aubrey seems to be so, much to his wife's dismay. But even my cousin is not as bad as Mr. Malvern. He visited us for nearly an hour today, and in that time I believe he detailed the pedigree of every dog in his pack. Fortunately, he had not time to go into his horses.''

They all laughed. ''Uncle thinks hunting is barbarous,'' said Geordie, causing the baron to color slightly

''Barbarous, Lord Ramsay?'' said Olivia.

He nodded. ''I do, ma'am. I do not think it sport for a hundred hounds to pursue one small fox. Nor do I think it sport for scores of huntsmen to ride wildly about the countryside, destroying everything in sight.''

Olivia frowned slightly. ''The hunt is hardly Napoleon's army, my lord. There is sport in racing one's horse across a field, taking all obstacles. And oftentimes, the fox escapes.''

''Only to provide entertainment for another hunt,'' said Ramsay coolly.

Rather alarmed at how Olivia and the baron were regarding each other, Burry hastened to change the subject. They then talked of less controversial topics, beginning with the weather and concluding with the historical research being done by the baron and Professor Burry. Ramsay was surprised to find that Olivia appeared so interested in the professor's description of his latest findings. However, knowing that the lady had doubtless been well-schooled in the art of conversation, he suspected the sincerity of Olivia's attentiveness.

After they had finished dinner, Olivia and Geordie left the gentlemen to their port and retired to the drawing room. Geordie was delighted to have Olivia to himself. He pushed the bath chair to a place near the sofa and Olivia transferred herself onto it. Geordie then sat down beside her. The dogs, having been banished from the dining room, were happy to have human company. Mayflower jumped up on the couch and curled up between them. The mastiff Wolstan had to be content placing his huge head on Olivia's lap.

"It was a delightful dinner, Geordie," said Olivia. "You have an excellent cook. I have scarcely eaten so well in London."

"I shall tell Cook you enjoyed her meal. She will be very pleased." Georgie petted the whippet and smiled at Olivia. "It must be very exciting in London, is it not, Lady Olivia?"

"At times it is," she replied. "There is so much to do there, and so many interesting and amusing people. One may attend parties, and then there are always ladies and gentlemen calling."

"I fancy I would like to go to parties," said Geordie wistfully.

"Surely there are parties here for young ladies and gentlemen."

Geordie shook his head. "None to which I am invited."

"Then you must have one here at Hawkesmuir and ask all your friends to come."

"I do not actually have any friends, Lady Olivia," returned the boy. "No one ever calls at Hawkesmuir Castle."

"Well, I shall call often, and so will Sir Aubrey and Lady Roxbury. And you must call upon us at Fenwyck."

"Oh, I should very much like to do so, Lady Olivia."

"Then tell me how you amuse yourself here, Geordie. Do you play games?"

"Sometimes, but mostly I read."

"That is good pastime. My nephew Ralph loves to read and he is about your age. I suspect you enjoy the same books. His favorite is *Robinson Crusoe*."

"I have not read that," said Geordie.

Olivia appeared surprised. "Then I shall get you a copy. But why don't you bring me your favorite book and I shall read it to you."

"Oh, I should like that very much," said Geordie. "I shall fetch it for you from the library." The boy rose from the couch and hurried from the drawing room. He returned a short time later with a heavy volume. Sitting down on the sofa, Geordie handed Olivia the book.

"It appears to be a very large book, Geordie," she said, and then, opening it to the title page, she read the title and author's name in some surprise. "*The Age of Chivalry,* by Lord Ramsay of Hawkesmuir. Why, your uncle has written this book."

The boy smiled proudly. "Uncle Gervas wrote it, every word. It is a very good book and Professor Burry says it is brilliant. I think it is exciting, especially the parts about battles." To Geordie's great satisfaction, Olivia appeared very impressed. "My uncle is a very clever man."

"Yes, I'm sure he is, to have written such a book," said Olivia, thumbing through the volume with great interest.

"Do you like my uncle, Lady Olivia?" asked Geordie.

Olivia smiled. "Yes, of course."

"Don't you think him handsome?"

"Yes, very handsome and quite charming."

Geordie beamed and Olivia was tempted to laugh at his expression. "I'm sure he likes you, Lady Olivia." He hesitated a moment. "You are not married, are you, ma'am?"

Olivia laughed. "No, I am not. Now, why don't I read you Lord Ramsay's book? You may select a particularly exciting passage."

Geordie took the book, and quickly turning to a chapter, handed it back to her. Olivia smiled once more and began to read.

When a short time later the baron and Professor Burry entered the drawing room, they witnessed a charming domestic scene. Lady Olivia was seated upon the sofa reading aloud to Geordie, who, listening with rapt attention, was sitting beside her. The mastiff was lying at their feet and the little whippet was on the couch, her head on her mistress's lap.

Noticing the gentlemen's entrance, Olivia stopped reading. "Oh, do go on, ma'am," said Geordie. "Uncle and the professor will not mind."

"Indeed not," said Burry, sitting down in a chair. "I should like a good story."

Olivia smiled at the baron. "Do you mind if I go on, Lord Ramsay? I am at a particularly exciting part."

His lordship shrugged, and sat down. "Very well, ma'am," he said.

Olivia continued, and Ramsay, immediately recognizing his own words, reddened. After Olivia read a few sentences describing the technique of using a broadsword, the baron interrupted her. "Perhaps that is enough reading, Lady Olivia, " he said.

"But, uncle," protested Geordie, "the next part is—"

"I know what the next part is. You cannot wish to bore Lady Olivia."

"It is scarcely boring, my lord," said Olivia with a smile.

The baron looked embarrassed. "Why don't you return the book to the library, Geordie?"

"But I was hoping you might allow me to borrow it,

Lord Ramsay,'' said Olivia. ''Truly, I think it very fascinating.''

Suspecting she was mocking him, Ramsay frowned. ''You may borrow it if you wish.''

''Thank you. How proud you must be to have written such a book.'' Olivia looked over at Burry. ''And you must be proud of your former pupil, sir.''

''Indeed I am, Lady Olivia. I never had a student more clever than his lordship.''

''Really, Professor,'' said the baron.

''Do not be overly modest, my boy. You know very well that yours is the best book ever to have been written on the subject.'' Burry nodded at Olivia. ''It is a remarkable feat of scholarship and I am consumed with envy to think that his lordship has written it at such a young age. If he had been truly grateful to his old professor, he might have put my name upon it.''

Olivia laughed and closed the book. ''Well, I shall read it myself later. And seeing how praise embarrasses Lord Ramsay, I shall say nothing further about it.''

''Lady Olivia has promised to visit us often from Fenwyck and will bring Sir Aubrey and Lady Roxbury as well,'' said Geordie, obviously very pleased at the prospect. ''And did you know, uncle,'' continued the boy, ''that Lady Olivia is not married?''

''I was aware of that,'' said the baron.

Geordie grinned at Olivia. ''You know, ma'am, when I first saw Uncle bring you in, I thought that perhaps he had brought home a wife.''

''Geordie!'' cried the baron.

Olivia laughed again. ''Do not terrify his lordship with such an idea.''

Professor Burry laughed heartily. ''Well, I think it a dashed pity that that was not the case.''

''Now you terrify Lady Olivia, Professor,'' said the baron. They all laughed, and Ramsay, hoping to keep his nephew from causing him further embarrassment, asked

Geordie to play the piano for their visitor. The boy was happy to oblige, giving a virtuoso performance of a Haydn piece. Olivia, very impressed with his musical talent, praised him highly. Then, noting that it was growing late, Ramsay announced that it was time for Geordie to go to bed. Realizing that she was tired from the day's adventure, Olivia said that she, too, would retire.

Although Olivia voiced a protest that it was unnecessary, the baron was adamant about carrying her. Finding herself once again in Ramsay's arms, Olivia realized that she did not mind at all. The baron said nothing as they made their way up the stairs and then continued to Olivia's room. Once inside, the baron gently placed her on the bed. "I shall send a maid to you, Lady Olivia," he said, turning to go.

"Lord Ramsay?" He stopped and looked at her. "I know you think me frivolous, and I do admit that I am not always serious. It is my nature to make light of things, but I want you to believe that I am not quizzing you when I praise your book. I think it quite remarkable and wonderfully written."

Ramsay was rather taken aback by the sincerity of her tone. Looking into Olivia's enormous blue eyes, the baron suddenly felt it was dangerous to remain there in the bedchamber with the beautiful Olivia. "Thank you," he said, and then, wishing her good night, he hastily departed.

11

Lady Roxbury smiled as she looked out the bedchamber window. "I think it is going to be a lovely day, Aubrey. Oh, how good it is to see the sun." There was no reply from the recumbent form of the baronet, who appeared still to be sleeping in the canopied bed. Turning away from the window, Sophie went over to her husband. "Aubrey," she said in a louder voice, "do not be such a slugabed."

Sir Aubrey opened his eyes and regarded his wife sleepily. "Is it not dreadfully early, dearest?"

"Perhaps it is early for town, but certainly not for the country. I daresay I could not sleep for thinking about Livy."

The baronet sat up in bed and presented a ludicrous picture with his nightcap askew on his unruly red hair. "Poor Livy," said Aubrey. "I suppose we must go and rescue her. I shall get up and we will make haste to go and fetch her."

Sophie sat down on the bed beside her husband and regarded him as if he were quite cork-brained. "We shall do nothing of the kind, my dear." Sir Aubrey looked puzzled and Sophie laughed and continued. "Ramsay said he would bring Livy back, and we must allow him to do so. Indeed, this is all too perfect! I know he cannot withstand her charm. We shall win the wager after all.''

''The wager?'' said the baronet. ''I thought you had called it off.''

''I am so glad I never said anything to Reggie about it. I shall so enjoy beating my brother.''

Sir Aubrey directed a skeptical look at his wife. ''But Ramsay is such an odd fellow. Do not be so confident, my sweet.''

''Do not be such an old puss, Aubrey,'' said Sophie, giving her husband a playful pat. ''Now, do get up. We must take advantage of such rare good weather.''

The baronet nodded and threw aside the bedcovers. ''Poor Livy,'' he said, ''she is undoubtedly miserable.'' His wife made no reply, but cheerfully rang for the servants.

Sir Aubrey would have been very much surprised to find how inaccurate were his words, for his cousin Olivia was at that moment having a most enjoyable time. Having just completed a delicious breakfast, that lady was now seated in the drawing room of Hawkesmuir Castle laughing at one of Professor Burry's remarks. Next to her sat Geordie, grinning happily. The baron stood by the fireplace regarding them all with a slight smile.

''Uncle Gervas,'' said Geordie, ''could we give Lady Olivia a tour of the castle and grounds?''

''I would like that, Lord Ramsay.'' said Olivia.

His lordship nodded. ''Very well.''

''But, Ramsay,'' said Professor Burry, ''it is time for Geordie's lessons.''

The boy's disappointed expression was comical and he looked imploringly at his uncle, who smiled. ''I believe, Professor Burry, that you might delay Geordie's morning lessons for a time.''

''Oh, thank you, uncle!'' exclaimed Geordie, hurrying to his feet. ''I shall push you in the bath chair, Lady Olivia.''

Olivia smiled. "You gentlemen are spoiling me."

Geordie hurried to fetch the chair. They were followed by the dogs as they proceeded from the drawing room and began the tour. After seeing several impressive and interesting rooms and listening to Professor Burry discourse on the history of Hawkesmuir Castle, Geordie suggested they go outside to see the castle gardens and stables. The lad ran off to get Olivia's shawl and a blanket, and after receiving repeated assurances that she was warm enough, they went outside.

Pleasantly surprised to find the morning air warmer than expected, the gentlemen and Olivia went into the garden. Despite the lateness of the season, the garden still retained its beauty and Olivia proclaimed it lovely indeed.

After lingering there for some time, Geordie was eager to go to the stables. "You do like horses, Lady Olivia?" said the boy, pushing the bath chair across the garden.

"Very much," said Olivia.

"I have been told that her ladyship is an excellent horsewoman," said the baron.

"Then you must come riding with Uncle and me as soon as your ankle will allow it," said Geordie.

"I would very much like to do that, Geordie," replied Olivia.

Coming to a large fenced pasture, Geordie stopped. "There are some of the horses, Lady Olivia. Look, there is Destre! He is Uncle's favorite."

Olivia watched the black stallion run across the pasture. She glanced over at the baron. "I believe I made Destre's acquaintance yesterday."

Ramsay smiled and then, to Olivia's surprise, whistled loudly. The big horse stopped, pricked up his ears, and then ran to them. "There's a good lad, Destre," said the baron, patting the horse affectionately.

"I have never seen such a large horse, Lord Ramsay."

"He is more than seventeen hands," said the baron, evidently proud of the stallion's great size.

Olivia looked from Destre to the mares that were also in the enclosure. "They are also very big," she said.

"That is because they have the blood of the medieval charger, ma'am," said Burry. "His lordship has bred them to be like the war horses of King Richard's day."

Olivia smiled over at Ramsay. "The age of chivalry, my lord?"

The baron looked a trifle embarrassed. "You must pardon my eccentric hobby, Lady Olivia."

"But I think it is wonderful. Why, I can easily imagine them with armored knights on their backs doing battle against the Saracens. Or I can picture a joust with knights of the Round Table."

"Lady Olivia," cried Geordie excitedly, "you must see Uncle joust!"

Olivia turned once again to the baron and raised her eyebrows with mock astonishment. "Indeed, my lord! Are you Sir Lancelot or Sir Galahad? I am eager to see you in your armor."

Ramsay reddened and Geordie replied, "Oh, he does not wear armor, Lady Olivia. And it is not actually a real joust. But he does take his lance against the target!"

"And he is dashed proficient at it," said Burry proudly. "Why, I daresay he could have held his own on Richard's Crusade."

"Please, sir," said the baron, "must you spout such fustian? Come, I am sure that Lady Olivia wishes to see the other horses."

"I shall not let you off so easily, my lord," said Olivia. "I insist that you demonstrate your jousting ability."

"Oh, please do so, Uncle Gervas," said Geordie.

"It is a splendid idea, Ramsay," said the professor. "You must show the lady how it is done."

"I don't think so," said the baron, frowning.

"But I insist upon it," returned Olivia, "and I shall continue badgering you until you submit."

Ramsay, thinking the lady was making sport of him,

scowled, and Olivia was reminded of how he appeared at the British Museum. "I cannot be quailed by your bearlike expression, my lord," said Olivia, "and I shall not leave Hawkesmuir Castle until I see your jousting. Be reasonable, Lord Ramsay, or I shall establish permanent residency here."

"Very well," replied the baron glumly. He shouted for a servant. "Jem, saddle Destre with the jousting saddle." The burly youth, who had been watching from the stable door, hurried out, apparently eager to do so. Grasping the big horse by the halter, Jem led the animal from the pasture into the stable.

"We must go to the jousting field, Lady Olivia," said Geordie, pushing the bath chair once again.

Although the idea of a jousting field struck Olivia as very amusing, she tried hard to keep from laughing. She watched Ramsay stalk off to the stables as Geordie wheeled her away.

The baron cursed as he entered the stable. Why had he submitted to this preposterous display? He imagined Olivia telling her London friends about it. How she would laugh at the eccentric baron who thought himself a medieval knight. He stood impatiently while Jem readied the horse. The servant was rather puzzled by his master's ill humor. Jem thought the baron would be pleased at the opportunity to show his skill before the beautiful and noble lady. Despite Jem Miller's rough exterior, the stableman had a romantic turn of mind. He had often imagined himself squire to the gallant knight, and Jem thought the addition of a lovely maiden as a spectator most welcome.

"Destre is ready, m'lord," said Jem.

The baron nodded and then climbed nimbly up into the old-fashioned saddle. Jem ran over and hurried back with a lance and a shield emblazoned with the baron's coat of arms. "I shall dispense with the shield today, Jem," he said. The stableman looked rather disappointed, for he thought his lordship's shield quite splendid.

Riding his charger out into the sunlight, the baron felt utterly ridiculous. He reluctantly directed his steed to the jousting field. The stallion pranced eagerly, knowing he would have an opportunity to run.

Olivia sat in the bath chair between Burry and Geordie and watched the baron ride out into the field. Noting the wicked-looking lance he was carrying, she smiled, "I'm sure it is fortunate his lordship has no opponent."

"No one would be so foolish as to go against Uncle Gervas," said Geordie.

"Indeed not," said Burry. He gestured toward the field in which was a series of posts set into the ground at long intervals. On each post stood a metal ring. "Norman knights were trained in this fashion" explained the professor. "The horseman must pick up the rings with his lance while riding full gallop."

Olivia eyed the rings and judged that to do as Professor Burry said would be a most difficult feat. She looked expectantly at Ramsay.

The baron's face was grim as he surveyed the field. Suddenly he spurred the stallion and raced toward the posts. Destre's great hooves thundered across the ground, and arriving within seconds at the first post, Ramsay lowered his lance and neatly hooked the ring. The stallion did not break stride as the baron urged him ahead toward the next object and again easily speared the ring. Olivia watched him in amazement as he continued to snatch up each ring, giving a flawless performance.

Geordie cheered loudly and Burry nodded. "By Jove, that was splendid. He did not miss even one."

Having concluded his feat of equestrian prowess, the baron rode Destre back to where Burry and Geordie were standing beside Olivia. He carried his lance upright, with all the rings stacked around it.

"Well done, Sir Knight," said Olivia, smiling up at him. She pulled a lace-trimmed handkerchief from her sleeve and held it toward him. "Do accept this small token of a lady's tribute."

He met her gaze, and then, finding nothing mocking in it, the baron smiled. "My lady is most kind," he said, taking the handkerchief and bowing from his saddle.

Burry, who was watching them closely, was quite delighted at the look Olivia and the baron exchanged. Geordie, too, was very pleased to see that his uncle had so impressed the lady. "Uncle Gervas, you must do it again. I shall have Jem put the rings back."

"I think once was quite enough, Geordie. I believe it is time you and the professor took Lady Olivia back into the house."

The boy looked a trifle disappointed but nodded. He then started to push Olivia's chair back toward the castle while Ramsay rode back to the stable. The dogs, who had been obediently sitting with the spectators during the exhibition, ran eagerly after the horse.

"I think your uncle is quite remarkable, Geordie," said Olivia.

"Oh yes," replied the boy enthusiastically, "and he looked very handsome, too. Didn't you think so, Lady Olivia?"

Olivia laughed. "Oh, yes, he looked very handsome."

Very happy with this reply, the boy continued to push her to the house. They went to the library, where the professor pointed out some of his lordship's prized books. A short time later the baron, with the dogs at his heels, joined them. "Uncle, we were just showing Lady Olivia your books."

"Well, young sir," said the professor, "we had best leave the rest of that to your uncle. It is time you had your lessons. To the schoolroom with you."

Geordie, thinking it a very good idea for his uncle to be alone with Lady Olivia, made no protest. Taking his leave of them, he followed Burry from the room.

When they had gone, Olivia smiled up at the baron. "I

think your nephew the dearest boy. You have done an admirable job in raising him.''

Ramsay shrugged. ''He has succeeded in spite of me. I fear I have been a poor substitute for his parents.''

''Nonsense. It is clear he adores you. I am surprised that he is not at school. I would have thought he would be at Eton like my oldest nephew.''

The baron frowned. ''After my experience there, Lady Olivia, I am not so eager to send him.''

''You disliked it so much?''

''I abhorred it.''

''But don't you ever worry, my lord,'' said Olivia, ''that Geordie has no companions of his own age?''

''Better no companions than bad ones.''

Olivia shook her head. ''You have little faith in young gentlemen, Lord Ramsay. I am sure there are many nice young boys who would make Geordie good friends. Perhaps there are some living in the area.''

''I would not know,'' replied the baron curtly.

Deciding it would be best to drop the subject, Olivia asked Ramsay to be seated. ''Your library is most impressive, my lord.''

Sitting down near her, the baron looked over at Olivia. ''I did not mean to force you to change the subject. It is just that I have little to do with local society. I rarely see anyone. Indeed, I am thought to be a recluse.''

''But I do not understand why that would be so.''

''It is because I prefer it that way. I know you find that singular.'' He smiled slightly. ''Indeed, I can imagine what you must think of me after my jousting exhibition.''

Olivia smiled. ''I think that you are an extraordinary horseman, Lord Ramsay. No, I am not gammoning you. I daresay directing a lance against a target is an unusual way to demonstrate your horsemanship, but I would not doubt that if gentlemen from town had seen you, it would soon become the rage. I think the Prince Regent would love the idea. Of course, his royal highness would insist on appearing in full armor."

Ramsay laughed. "That is a daunting prospect indeed."

"But I do hope your dislike of society will not prevent you from visiting us at Fenwyck. And do say you will admit us if we call. I should like to visit again at Hawkesmuir Castle."

"You will be more than welcome here," said the baron softly, and Olivia was somewhat disconcerted by the expression in his dark eyes.

"Thank you, my lord," she managed to say, and then, feeling rather awkward, glanced about the room. Noting a picture of a horse, she remarked upon it. "That is a fine painting. A Stubbs, is it not?"

Ramsay nodded. "My father commissioned it years ago. It is a portrait of his favorite hunter, Hercules." Noting Olivia's expression, the baron felt an explanation was necessary. "My father loved hunting. Each year he could hardly bear to wait until November when the season started. Each year at this time I think of him." He looked over at her. "I'm sure you are wondering why I do not share my father's passion for the hunt."

"I own it is unusual to find a gentleman who does not enjoy hunting."

"It's odd, but I never did, even as a small boy. I always had a curious empathy for the fox. When I was younger than Geordie, I witnessed a kill and saw the hounds tear the fox apart. I knew I never wanted to see that again, nor have any part in a hunt."

"Did your father accept this?"

He smiled slightly and shook his head. "He could not imagine having a son so fainthearted and always hoped I would come to my senses." He smiled again. "I never have, it seems."

Olivia regarded him sympathetically. "It cannot have been easy for you if your father was at all like mine. He lived for hunting and was so disappointed that my brother,

Edward, showed no inclination for the sport. I think that is why he always encouraged me to hunt, even though it is not considered at all the thing for a female to do so.'' She smiled. ''Poor Papa. I think he always wished that I was another son.''

''Well, I am glad that he had a daughter,'' said the baron. Olivia had not expected this remark and regarded him in some surprise. The baron colored slightly and somewhat abruptly changed the subject. Olivia regarded him in some amusement, but obligingly began to discuss his book collection.

12

An old, much-traveled open carriage pulled up in front of Fenwyck, causing several of the servants to peer out the window curiously. The object of their interest was the tenth Baron Ramsay of Hawkesmuir, a gentleman they considered a very mysterious personage. Although most of the servants had lived their entire lives in the vicinity, few had ever seen Ramsay. The news that the beautiful Lady Olivia had spent the night at Hawkesmuir Castle had provoked much comment belowstairs. After watching the baron jump down from the carriage, one of the maids hurried to the drawing room, where Aubrey and Sophie were sitting. "Lady Olivia has returned, m'lady!" she exclaimed.

"Poor girl," said Aubrey, glancing at the clock. "She had to spend most of the day with the fellow. It is past four o'clock!"

"I think it bodes very well. If she had been miserable, she would have insisted upon coming home sooner." Sophie smiled. "Let us meet them at the entry hall. Come along, Aubrey."

The baronet followed his wife out of the room and they arrived in the entry hall just as the butler opened the door.

There stood Ramsay with Olivia in his arms. A small boy was standing beside them with a book clutched in his hands, and all of them were laughing. The whippet Mayflower was there too, looking adoringly up at her mistress.

Aubrey stood dumbfounded, but Lady Roxbury rushed to greet them. "My poor Livy, are you all right?"

"Oh, yes, I am fine. Lord Ramsay insists on carrying me, although I have assured him repeatedly that I am no invalid."

Sophie smiled at the baron. "How very gallant of you, Lord Ramsay. Do bring Livy in."

They all went into the drawing room and Ramsay placed Olivia down on the sofa. Aubrey, who had by now regained his powers of speech, grinned at his cousin. "I hope you don't expect me to carry you about like that, Livy. I don't think I could manage it."

Olivia laughed. "Do not fear, Aubrey, I shall not ask that of you. Indeed, I know I shall be able to get about by myself."

"We are so grateful to you, Lord Ramsay," said Sophie. "How fortunate you were there to find Livy." Noticing Geordie, she smiled at the boy. "And who is this little gentleman?"

"This is my nephew, George Sinclair, Lady Roxbury. Geordie, may I present Lady Roxbury and Sir Aubrey?"

Geordie bowed politely. "How do you do?"

"Do sit down, gentlemen," said the baronet affably. "I hope you will stay to tea."

The baron glanced over at Geordie and, seeing his nephew's eager expression, nodded. "That is very kind, Roxbury." They all sat down. Mayflower jumped up beside Olivia and curled up against her.

"Now, Livy" said Sophie, "do tell us all about your adventure. How horrid it must have been to fall!"

"I do not know what I would have done if the baron had not come."

"I did tell you not to go very far," said Sir Aubrey disapprovingly. "Now perhaps you will be more careful."

"Aubrey, how unkind of you to chide Livy," said Sophie. "You must just be thankful that she was close to Hawkesmuir Castle and did not come to harm."

"Yes, yes," said the baronet, "I am thankful for that."

Sophie looked over at Geordie and noted that he was holding a book in his lap. "And what is that, Mr. Sinclair?"

"A book for Lady Olivia, ma'am."

"How wonderful," returned Sophie. "I do hope it is a new novel. I have nothing to read here except . . ." She paused and looked over at her husband. ". . . the most dreadful book on household management."

"I fear it is not a novel," said Olivia, smiling at the baron, "but it is just as exciting. It is called *The Age of Chivalry,* and Lord Ramsay is the author."

"The devil you say," said Sir Aubrey. "Might I see that, young man?" When Geordie handed him the book, the baronet thumbed through it. "I daresay it is a lot of words, Ramsay."

"Yes, quite a few," said the baron.

"Of course," said Sophie, "Lord Ramsay is a scholar. We met him in the British Museum."

"Did you, ma'am?" asked Geordie. "Oh, how I should like to go there."

"It was deuced interesting," said Aubrey. "I saw the most enormous beetle. Such an ugly fellow he was!"

Olivia suppressed a laugh. "Yes, the insects are well worth seeing, but I was more interested in the de Courcy manuscript." She looked over at the baron. "His lordship knows that I am an expert on it." Ramsay smiled and Olivia continued, "When you visit London, Geordie, I shall take you to the British Museum."

Geordie appeared thrilled. "How I would like that, Lady Olivia."

"Then we will simply have to persuade your uncle to bring you to town in the spring."

Geordie's face fell. "Uncle does not like London. He says that all who live there are fops and reprobates."

Sophie, Aubrey, and Olivia all directed inquisitive looks at the baron, who looked rather uncomfortable. "Indeed, my lord?" said Olivia. "And which am I?"

"But a lady cannot be a fop," said Geordie seriously.

The others all burst into laughter. "Perhaps I am a trifle harsh," said Ramsay, smiling sheepishly. "In any case, I shall guard my words with this young man about."

Rather worried that he had committed a faux pas, Geordie was relieved that his uncle did not seem angry with him. Indeed, the baron appeared to be in an excellent mood as the conversation continued.

After a most enjoyable tea, Ramsay and his nephew took their leave and were soon on their way back to Hawkesmuir Castle. As the equipage traveled down the graveled lane, Geordie turned back to look at Fenwyck. "That was such fun, uncle. I did like Lady Roxbury very much. She was quite pretty and so kind. And I thought Sir Aubrey a pleasant gentleman. Did you not think his clothes splendid, uncle?"

Ramsay looked over at his nephew in some surprise. In truth, the baron had thought Sir Aubrey's striped coat outlandish and his mustard-colored pantaloons ludicrous. "I fear I do not share Sir Aubrey's taste in dress. I do not believe a gentleman should be confused with a peacock."

The boy considered this. "Then is Sir Aubrey a fop?"

"I would not say so. However, I will admit that Sir Aubrey pays a good deal more attention to his clothes than I do."

Geordie glanced at his uncle. "But then, don't most gentlemen?"

Ramsay burst into laughter. "Yes, you rascal. I can see you think me very shabby beside Sir Aubrey."

The boy hesitated before replying. "You are much handsomer," he said tactfully, "and your new clothes are quite as nice as Sir Aubrey's, although not nearly so colorful. How splendid it would be to have such fine clothes.''

"So you think your clothes not up to snuff, nephew?''

Geordie looked down at his sleeves, which were too short, and then glanced back at the baron. "Oh, no, uncle, I am sure they are fine.''

"I must disagree, Geordie. I believe I have been remiss in seeing to your wardrobe. We must remedy the situation immediately. How would you like to go to Newcastle upon Tyne tomorrow and see a proper tailor?''

"Oh, Uncle Gervas, that would be famous. Could I get a striped coat like Sir Aubrey's?''

"Not quite like Sir Aubrey's,'' said the baron, "but do not fear, you will be none the less stylish.''

"Maybe Lady Olivia would like to come with us,'' suggested Geordie.

"I think, Geordie, that we gentlemen should do this alone.''

"Yes, you are right, uncle. But we will see Lady Olivia again soon, won't we?''

"I am sure we will,'' returned the baron, trying to sound indifferent.

"I did like her very much,'' said Geordie. "Didn't you?''

"I scarcely know the lady,'' replied the baron.

His nephew appeared disappointed with this answer. "But she likes you. She said she thought you were handsome and charming.''

"That is bosh, Geordie.''

"It is the truth. And she said you are a remarkable horseman.''

"She was simply being polite.''

Although somewhat frustrated by his uncle's responses, Geordie was about to make another remark about Lady Olivia when he spied a horseman coming toward them. "Look, uncle, it is Mr. Malvern.''

The baron frowned as he, too, saw the squire approaching astride a magnificent bay horse. Ever since Ramsay had been a boy, he had despised Roger Malvern. Two years the baron's senior, young Malvern had been the bane of Ramsay's childhood. Malvern and his followers, a group of village boys, had delighted in taunting the youthful Ramsay about his limp. There was irony in that most of his former tormentors were now very deferential to the baron on the rare occasions when they happened to meet him. Indeed, his lordship was sure that they very much regretted their earlier behavior to a rich and powerful landowner. The squire, however, had not changed. Ever contemptuous and jealous of Ramsay's wealth and title, he remained disdainful. The baron, in turn, treated Malvern with a lordly condescension that infuriated Malvern.

Adopting his most arrogant expression, Ramsay ignored the squire and would have passed by him, had not Malvern hailed the carriage, making the driver pull to a stop. "Ramsay," said the squire, bringing his horse alongside the equipage.

"Malvern," returned his lordship icily.

The squire directed a scornful look at the carriage. "They certainly made good carriages in your grandfather's day."

The baron seemed to take no note of this remark. "If you have something to say to me, Malvern, I suggest you do so and quit wasting my time."

"I crave your lordship's pardon." Malvern sneered. "I see you have come from Fenwyck. I heard you had met the Roxburys and Lady Olivia in London. We are fortunate in having such beauties as neighbors. But what is so damned curious is that Lady Olivia seems so enamored of you, Ramsay."

"What are you talking about?"

The squire grinned. "When I met her yesterday, she talked about you. By God, from her description, I would not have recognized you. I decided that either you are a very different man in London or the lady is in dire need of a rich husband. I shall endeavor to find out which is the case. And I do hate to disappoint you, Ramsay, but after the wench becomes better acquainted with me, I daresay she won't settle for you.'' Not allowing the baron time to reply, Malvern kicked his horse and rode off.

Geordie looked over at his uncle, expecting to find Lord Ramsay very upset. To his surprise, the baron smiled and was in the best of moods all the way home.

13

The baron and Geordie had scarcely left when Sir Aubrey turned eagerly to his cousin. "Tell us, Livy," he said, "was it truly dreadful?"

Olivia laughed. "It was not in the least dreadful. Indeed, I had such a lovely time. Lord Ramsay, Geordie, and Professor Burry could not have been kinder to me."

"Professor Burry?" said Sophie. "Who is he?"

"He is Geordie's tutor and quite a likable gentleman."

"You amaze me, cousin," drawled the baronet. "You spend an evening and the good part of the day in the company of a schoolmaster, a small boy, and a monk and you have a lovely time. I find it most curious."

"Perhaps, Aubrey, the baron is not the monk he is thought to be," said Sophie. She directed a mischievous smile at Olivia. "What do you think, Livy?" Olivia blushed and her friend laughed. "Good heavens! You have a *tendre* for him!"

"Don't be ridiculous," said Olivia unconvincingly.

"You cannot be fond of him, Livy!" cried Aubrey. "I grant that he is rich, and I will say his clothes today were quite presentable, but he has nothing else to commend him. I don't find him the least amusing, and he scribbles dry old tomes!"

"His book is not in the least dull, Aubrey," protested Olivia. "I think he is the most fascinating man I have ever met."

"Good God," muttered Aubrey, "and the fellow don't even hunt!"

Olivia did not have opportunity to reply, for the butler entered the room and announced that Squire Malvern had arrived. Aubrey appeared very happy at this intelligence, and instructed the servant to hasten and show the gentleman to the drawing room.

Malvern came through the door looking massive and well pleased with himself. He bowed to the ladies, and Sir Aubrey rose and shook his hand. "How good to see you, Malvern," he said. "Do sit down."

The big man smiled amiably at Sir Aubrey and tried to mask the scorn he had for the baronet's appearance. He considered Roxbury a fool and a coxcomb and would have had nothing to do with him had it not been for Sir Aubrey's wealth. The Malvern Hunt was in dire need of a rich patron, and the squire, although despising his new neighbor, was happy to take his money for the support of the hunt.

Malvern took a seat near Olivia. "I see I was not your only visitor," he said. "I met Ramsay in your lane. He was in that antique carriage of his." He directed a meaningful glance at Olivia. "It goes to show that just because a fellow has blunt, it don't mean he'll spend it. There is no more hard-fisted man in the kingdom."

"I cannot believe that, Mr. Malvern," said Olivia, frowning disapprovingly at the squire. "When I was at Hawkesmuir, I was most impressed with the furnishings. They were tasteful and quite modern. If Lord Ramsay were a miser, the castle would have been furnished with worn-out relics."

"You were at Hawkesmuir Castle?" said Malvern in surprise.

"I spent the night there," replied Olivia matter-of-factly.

Malvern looked over at Aubrey. "You stayed at Ramsay's house last night?"

"No, just Livy." The baronet hastened to explain. "She was out walking and met with a slight accident. She fell and sprained her ankle and Ramsay found her and took her to Hawkesmuir Castle."

"And I thoroughly enjoyed myself," added Olivia.

Noting that his guest was looking disgruntled, the baronet turned the subject to horses. "My Irish hunters arrived this morning. They are beauties! You must see them."

Malvern seemed very interested. "Indeed, I must. Have you tried them?"

Aubrey nodded. "Noble bits of blood and bone they are, easy-gaited and strong. I cannot wait to test them in a hunt."

"You will not have long to wait, Roxbury. The first hunt will be in two weeks' time. Everyone is so excited, for there is no hunt in all of England like ours." Malvern grinned. "That is because there is no pack like mine." He laughed and then continued. "Of course, it will not be the same this year without the hunt ball. The ladies are disappointed, I must say."

"But why is there no hunt ball, Mr. Malvern?" asked Sophie.

"It was always held here at Fenwyck, ma'am, and now that the Wendells are gone, there is no one else willing to host it. Of course, I would do so, but I do not think planning balls the province of bachelors. I tried to convince my sister to do so, but Caroline does not like balls overmuch and refuses."

"It is a pity not to have a ball," said Aubrey.

Sophie nodded and then appeared to be struck with an idea. "Why don't we have the ball? Of course, perhaps everyone would think it presumptuous of us, since we are only newly arrived."

"Certainly not," said Malvern, pleased that his words had had the desired effect. Indeed, it had been his purpose in coming there to get Sir Aubrey to host the ball, for the squire himself was unwilling to stand the expense of it. "Everyone will be most grateful to you. How splendid it would be to have another ball at Fenwyck."

"It will be such fun having the ball, will it not, Aubrey?" said Sophie eagerly.

"Oh, yes, my dear, but do you think you could arrange it on such short notice?" asked the baronet.

"I'm sure of it," replied Sophie, "but I will need Mr. Malvern's help to make the guest list. We know no one but you and Lord Ramsay."

Malvern smiled unpleasantly. "There is no need to send him an invitation, Lady Roxbury."

"And why is that?" asked Olivia.

"Because the man does not hunt, for one thing," returned the squire. "And for another, he would never attend a ball."

"I daresay we should have to invite him in any case," said Aubrey. "It would not look well if we did not."

"Do as you will, Roxbury," said the squire, "but you can be assured he will refuse."

Now that the matter of the ball was settled, Sir Aubrey suggested that Malvern come and see his new horses. Olivia quickly excused herself from venturing to the stables, saying her ankle would not allow it. Sophie, who had no great love for horses, also stayed behind.

When the gentlemen had left, Olivia turned to her friend. "I think Malvern is a detestable man."

"He is," agreed Sophie, "but Aubrey seems to like him and I fear we must rely on him to tell us whom to invite to the ball."

"I wish there was someone else on whom we could rely for that."

"But there is not, so we must tolerate him. But don't worry, my dear, we will invite Lord Ramsay first of all." Sophie looked closely at Olivia. "I hope he will come, for your sake. But you must tell me how you have come to

like him, since only a short time ago in town we both
thought him dreadful."

Olivia smiled. "He improves on further acquaintance."

Sophie regarded her friend skeptically. "I do hope so. I
must say it is really too funny that you like him, considering the wager. And since he now seems quite interested in
you, perhaps he will ask for you by Christmas."

Olivia directed a warning look at her friend. "Do not be
absurd."

"Why is it absurd? My dear girl, you have received
offers from almost every eligible man you have met. Surely
he is not different."

"But he is different," said Olivia thoughtfully. "Very
different from the other gentlemen I know."

Since Sophie had never considered being different a
virtue, she was still perplexed at the baron's appeal to
Olivia. However, she did not pursue the matter but began
to talk about the ball.

Sir Aubrey watched nervously while Squire Malvern
examined his new horses with a critical eye. When Malvern finally pronounced them good-looking beasts, the
baronet was relieved. "Aye," said the squire, "they'll
need testing in the field, but from the look of them, I
would say you've not been cheated, Roxbury."

"I am glad of your opinion, Malvern. I know you are a
good judge of horses."

The squire acknowledged the compliment with a nod.
"I'm a good judge of horses, hounds, and . . ." He
paused and grinned. ". . . women. But then, you are a
fair judge of females yourself, Roxbury, having found
such a lovely wife." The baronet appeared very pleased at
the remark. Malvern continued. "And your cousin is also
a fine-looking woman, although I cannot understand her
interest in a man like Ramsay."

"I daresay it is perplexing," replied Aubrey.

"Of course, he is rich and many females would think that reason enough to set their caps for him."

"Not Livy. She has turned down other wealthy suitors in town. Indeed, she does not care so much about a man's blunt. She doesn't have to. Her brother, the Marquess of Branford, is one of the richest men in the kingdom, and a substantial fortune will come to the man who marries her."

This information seemed of great interest to the squire. Olivia had already attracted Malvern with her beauty, but the knowledge that she would make her future husband wealthy made her even more desirable. The squire was not a rich man. Although his fortune was ample enough to support a comfortable country existence, it was hardly enough to sustain Malvern's profligate spending. The squire had spent vast sums on his hounds and horses, and his love of gaming was ruinous. Malvern knew that finding a wealthy wife would be a prudent move, and if such a wife were as beautiful as Lady Olivia, so much the better.

"I think your cousin deserves a man rather than that cold fish Ramsay," said the squire.

Aubrey smiled. "You could not have someone in mind, could you, Malvern?"

The squire laughed. "I could, indeed," he replied.

Both gentlemen laughed, and then they turned their attention back to the hunters.

14

The week following Olivia's return from Hawkesmuir was exceedingly busy for the residents of Fenwyck. Sophie and Olivia spent much time making arrangements for the ball. There were so many things to do and so little time. In addition, the word having passed that the new owners of Fenwyck were giving a hunt ball, they were besieged with callers anxious to secure invitations.

Olivia was rather disappointed that the baron was not among the many visitors to Fenwyck. She so often thought of Ramsay, but took his absence to mean that he was not thinking of her.

That morning Sophie and Olivia sat in the library attempting to finish the invitations before the inevitable callers would arrive in the afternoon. Sophie completed writing a name in her ornate style, and after blotting it, looked over at her friend. "If only I had a secretary. I daresay making out so many invitations is hard on one's hand."

"Well, I think that is the last one," said Olivia. "It does seem that the local society is much larger than I had expected."

Sophie nodded. "But Mr. Malvern assures me they are all very respectable. And, indeed, those we have met seem quite pleasant and not nearly so provincial as one might imagine."

Olivia smiled. "Did you think they would be quite uncivilized, Sophie?"

"Oh, I did not expect savages, of course, but then, I did not fancy they would be very polished. After all, we are so far north, nearly at the Scottish border."

Olivia eyed her friend with amusement. "We must be grateful that our neighbors are not barbarians, except Mr. Malvern, that is."

"Livy!" cried Sophie in mock disapproval. "How can you be so cruel to speak so of a man who is obviously smitten with you?"

"He is smitten with my fortune. That is very clear from his inquiries about my brother. I shall not forgive Aubrey for informing him of my situation."

"How cynical you are. At least you do not seem cynical about Lord Ramsay. I think you like him."

Olivia frowned slightly. "I'm sure he has quite forgotten me."

"Stuff. Of course he has not forgotten you. He is probably just busy with another book. I know he will call this afternoon." Sophie started to gather up her invitations. "I shall have the servants deliver these." Leafing through them, she stopped and pulled one from the pile. Handing it to Olivia, she smiled. "Why don't we deliver this one ourselves? Now that your ankle is completely recovered, you could use an outing."

Olivia looked down at the invitation and read Ramsay's name. "Since he has not called here, perhaps he does not want to see me."

"Why don't we find out?" suggested Sophie.

Olivia paused and then nodded. "Very well."

"Good," said her friend. "I certainly want to see his castle. I must have a servant fetch Aubrey from those horses of his, and we will go as soon as possible."

Aubrey, whose plans for the morning had not included a visit to Hawkesmuir Castle, was not overly enthusiastic at the idea of calling upon Ramsay. However, he submitted to his wife's coaxing, and the three of them set out for Hawkesmuir under a gray November sky.

The butler, who answered the door, seemed quite happy to see them. "How fortunate that you have called today," he said, "for his lordship just returned from Newcastle upon Tyne last evening. I shall tell his lordship that you are here."

When the servant had left, Sophie nudged her friend. "You see, that is why he did not call," she whispered.

"Newcastle?" said Aubrey. "Why would anyone go there?" The ladies eyed Aubrey but showed no inclination to speculate. Soon the butler returned and escorted them to the drawing room.

The baron greeted his guests politely and Sophie could not fail to note that Ramsay appeared very pleased to see her friend. After bidding them all to be seated, the baron turned to Olivia. "It appears your ankle is much better, ma'am."

Olivia nodded. "Yes, I am happy to inform you that you no longer have to carry me about."

Ramsay smiled. "Geordie will be so disappointed that he missed you. He and the professor have gone to the abbey ruins."

"Abbey ruins?" said Aubrey. "Poor lad, that sounds like a frightful bore."

"Not everyone is so easily bored as you, Aubrey," said Sophie.

The baronet nodded. "Yes, I have found that to be the case." He turned to Ramsay. "Your man said you were at Newcastle upon Tyne. Business, I suppose?"

"One might say that," replied the baron.

"I am so glad that we have found you at home, Lord Ramsay," said Sophie, "because we are here to deliver an invitation to you. We are having a hunt ball Thursday next."

"Yes," said Aubrey, "when Malvern said the Wendells always hosted a hunt ball at Fenwyck, we thought we should continue the tradition. Perhaps it is mad to do so in such little time, but my dear Sophie thought it could be done.''

Olivia noticed that the baron was looking down at the invitation with a decided lack of enthusiasm. ''I do hope you will come, Lord Ramsay,'' she said, smiling at him.

''I fear I do not attend balls, Lady Olivia,'' he replied bluntly, ''but I do thank you for the invitation.''

''But you simply must attend,'' protested Sophie. ''There is such a dearth of single gentlemen at balls. You cannot wish to disappoint all the ladies.''

Ramsay frowned. ''I shall disappoint no one in not attending, Lady Roxbury.''

Sophie regarded him in some surprise and Aubrey eyed him with disapproval. ''You will disappoint me, my lord,'' said Olivia, fastening her blue eyes upon his.

The baron was disconcerted by the earnestness of her expression, but managed to reply. ''I am sorry, but I shall not attend.''

''You cannot mean, Ramsay,'' said Aubrey, ''that not only do you dislike hunting, but you dislike balls as well?''

''I do mean it,'' returned Ramsay coolly.

The baron's reaction to the ball cast a pall on the conversation and Olivia's attempts to lighten the mood were unsuccessful. The visit seemed strained and awkward and Aubrey was eager to cut it short. ''I fear we must be going, Ramsay,'' said the baronet, rising from his chair. The ladies rose also and they took their leave.

Once in their carriage and on the road back to Fenwyck, Aubrey shook his head. '' 'Pon my honor, cousin, I found the man most uncivil. If the fellow did not want to go to the ball, why did he not have the good manners to simply send his regrets?''

''One must credit his honesty,'' said Olivia.

''I prefer good manners to honesty,'' said Aubrey irritably. ''Why, he acted as if attending our ball would be a horrible fate.''

''But I am sure it was not our ball,'' said Sophie. ''He

said he disliked balls in general.'' She turned to Olivia. ''I find disliking balls a serious fault in a gentleman.''

''And do not forget his disliking hunting,'' interjected Aubrey.

''I do not find that quite so serious a fault,'' said Lady Roxbury, smiling at her husband. ''But truly, Livy, I do not see that he has changed in any way. He seems the same man that he did in London.''

''Indeed so,'' said Aubrey. ''He does not deserve your notice, Livy. But Malvern is a dashed good fellow. I think you should show more interest in him.''

Olivia frowned. ''I caution you, Aubrey, do not try to encourage Malvern's attentions to me. I think him quite odious and do not care one fig that he may be the best master of hounds in England.''

Sophie and Aubrey exchanged a glance but said nothing further as the carriage made its way back toward Fenwyck.

The following morning Olivia rose early and dressed in her riding habit. Knowing that Aubrey and Sophie would not rise for some time, she went out to the stables, followed by Mayflower, and requested that a groom saddle a horse for her.

Starting down the lane that led from the house, Olivia held her horse to a decorous trot. The whippet ran ahead of the horse, happy to be out-of-doors. It was a crisp fall day and the sun peeked out occasionally from behind the clouds.

As she rode along, Olivia thought of Ramsay. She wondered why he was so opposed to attending the ball. His adamancy about not doing so had appeared very strange to Sophie and Aubrey. Doubtless he had his reasons, she decided, but Olivia thought the idea of attending the ball without him very dreary.

During her short stay at Hawkesmuir Castle, Olivia's feelings concerning the baron had radically changed. Indeed, she had found herself very much attracted to him, more so than any other man she had known.

Olivia continued on, thinking about Ramsay, until, arriving at a crossroads, she saw a dogcart approaching. Recognizing the driver as Professor Burry, she pulled her horse to a stop. Espying her, Burry waved in her direction. "Professor Burry," said Olivia, "how good to see you."

"Lady Olivia and the admirable Mayflower, this is indeed a pleasure. I do hope you are on your way to Hawkesmuir Castle."

Olivia shook her head. "No, sir, I was just out riding."

"Geordie was so disappointed that he missed your visit yesterday. Why don't you come with me now?"

"Oh, no, Professor, I don't think I could." She changed the subject. "And where were you, sir, at the ruined abbey again?"

"Why, yes, I was, Lady Olivia."

"Lord Ramsay told me that you and Geordie were there yesterday. I thought it sounded quite interesting. Is it nearby?"

"It is just two miles west of here. You must go out and see it. Indeed, you should ask Lord Ramsay to show it to you. He is the true expert on the abbey's history and has written of it in his book. He has studied it since he was a boy and he often told me it was his favorite haunt."

Olivia hesitated. "Professor Burry, you seem to know his lordship so very well. Do you know why he so dislikes society?"

Burry smiled slightly. "You are upset that he refused to go to your ball. He told me about the invitation. My dear Lady Olivia, you must understand Ramsay. His childhood was most unhappy and he has cause to distrust people."

"What do you mean, sir?"

"As a lad he was often ridiculed by other youths because he was not like them. You are aware, of course, of his limp?"

"Yes, but it is scarcely noticeable."

"Ramsay has told me that it was much worse when he was a boy. Having been afflicted from birth with a weakness in his leg, he was treated as an invalid. He was not allowed to run and play like other children and, therefore, he sought companionship in books. Fortunately, when Ramsay was older, his father discovered an excellent physician, a progressive man who helped to strengthen the lad's leg through a regimen of exercise.

"When I met him at Oxford, he was such a quiet and serious young man. Of course, his scholarship was quite remarkable, setting him above the rest. He had formed a protective shell about him and would not let others penetrate it." The professor paused and smiled. "Mrs. Burry was perhaps the first to break through his defenses. She was a remarkable woman, my Agatha. She liked Ramsay from the first and made an effort to draw him out. I will say, ma'am, that although his affection is not easily gained, once obtained, it is steadfast."

"I know he is very fond of you and devoted to Geordie," said Olivia. "But I wish he would give others the opportunity to be his friends. Professor, do you not think you could persuade him to go to the ball?"

Burry shook his head. "I don't believe so, Lady Olivia. But perhaps you could."

Olivia blushed. "I really don't think I could, sir."

"Well, why don't you accompany me to Hawkesmuir and attempt it?"

"I fear I must return to Fenwyck, but perhaps you could persuade Lord Ramsay to call upon me there."

Burry smiled. "Well, between Geordie and myself, I believe we could accomplish that."

"Good," said Olivia. She paused. "Do tell his lordship that I would very much like to see him again."

Professor Burry assured her that he would do so, and then Olivia turned her horse and started back toward Fenwyck.

15

Baron Ramsay sat in the library the following afternoon at an elegant cherry desk piled high with books. His brow furrowed in concentration, he dipped his quill pen in ink and started to write. After finishing a sentence, his pen halted and the baron appeared thoughtful. It was some time before he continued writing, adding a few more words before stopping once again.

"Damn," muttered Ramsay, frowning at the paper. The baron usually wrote very rapidly. Indeed, most of the time his pen could scarcely keep up with his thoughts. However, that afternoon his lordship found his usual facility distressingly impaired. It seemed he could not concentrate on his treatise on the reigns of the last Plantagenets.

The baron put down his pen in frustration and stared across the room at a tapestry hanging on the wall. A fine example of the medieval weaver's craft, it featured a lovely golden-haired maiden seated in a meadow with a unicorn, its horselike head resting on her lap. Studying the lady in the tapestry, he was suddenly struck by her resemblance to Olivia Dunbar. Ramsay shook his head, wondering if there was indeed a likeness or if it was just his addlepated fancy.

His lordship folded his arms across his chest and leaned back in his chair. Why could he not put her from his mind? he asked himself irritably. Since meeting her in London, Ramsay had thought of her with increasing frequency, until now Olivia dominated his reflections. Having always been immune to the charms of pretty women, the baron was annoyed to find himself as besotted as a lovesick medieval troubadour.

Ramsay opened a drawer of the desk and took out a lace-trimmed handkerchief. He raised it to his face and detected Olivia's delicate floral scent. The baron smiled wistfully for a moment, and then guiltily returned the handkerchief to the drawer.

Since it was quite apparent that Ramsay was not able to accomplish anything, he was glad when his nephew and Professor Burry appeared at the door of the library. "Do we disturb you, Ramsay?" said the professor.

"Oh, no, do come in."

Geordie eagerly entered the room. "Uncle Gervas, Professor Burry wants to tell you something."

The baron eyed Burry expectantly. "And what is that, sir?"

"It is this," he said, flourishing a paper in his hand and then giving it to Ramsay. "Master Sinclair has written a remarkable essay about the fall of Charles the First. I daresay it is the best work he has ever done."

Ramsay looked down at the paper and then smiled over at Geordie, who was beaming at the praise. "I am very proud of you, nephew. I shall read it and then we can spend the afternoon discussing your views."

"That would be very good, uncle," replied Geordie hesitantly, "but perhaps you could read it this evening and we could do something else this afternoon."

"Something else?"

The boy nodded. "Could we not go to Fenwyck and visit Lady Olivia?"

"That is a capital idea," said Burry. "The lad deserves

a free afternoon after such work. And as I told you, Lady Olivia is most anxious for you to call.''

Seeing that his uncle looked skeptical, Geordie hurried to interject, ''Oh, do say we might go, uncle. Please say yes.''

Ramsay paused and then shrugged with feigned indifference. ''Very well, if you wish.'' He looked at the professor. ''We can go right away.''

''As much as I would like to see the dear young lady,'' said Burry, ''I shall beg off. You know that I must work on my book.''

This remark brought a slight smile to the baron's face, for the professor had been working on the same book for more than forty years. ''If you are certain, sir?''

Burry nodded vigorously.

''Very well,'' said Ramsay, turning to his nephew. ''Go get ready, Geordie.''

The boy grinned and scurried out of the library.

The professor looked as if he were about to say something, but then seemed to think better of it. ''You must excuse me, Ramsay, but I should get to work. Do give my regards to Lady Olivia.''

The baron assured him he would do so, and Burry left the room, a knowing smile on his face.

The mantel clock in the drawing room at Fenwyck chimed and Olivia looked up, surprised at the lateness of the hour. She sat on the sofa, a book in her lap, Mayflower curled up beside her. Olivia had been very engrossed in *The Age of Chivalry* and it was now three o'clock. She had begun reading directly after luncheon, when Aubrey and Sophie had gone to pay a call on Malvern.

Aubrey had not been at all pleased by his cousin's refusal to accompany them, but Olivia had been adamant in her decision. She reflected that Aubrey was exasperatingly thickheaded in his inability to accept the fact that she could not abide that gentleman.

Olivia looked down at her book, and after marking her place carefully, she turned once again to the title page. Seeing Ramsay's name, she smiled. The baron had certainly written a fascinating book, as evidenced by her interest in it. Hitherto she had thought history a dull subject, but Ramsay's book brought the Middle Ages vividly to life.

Continuing to stare thoughtfully at the baron's name, Olivia remembered how he had ridden the charger Destre, lance in hand. She suddenly imagined him in armor with plumed helmet and shield, leading his knights into battle.

When sometime later a maid entered the room the servant found Olivia sitting on the sofa, a dreamy expression on her face, "Pardon me, m'lady."

Olivia looked startled. "Yes?"

"There are two gentlemen here, m'lady. Lord Ramsay and young Master Sinclair."

Olivia hoped she was not blushing at the mention of Ramsay's name. She had just been daydreaming that she was a medieval lady and Ramsay was her lord, returning to the castle after a long battle campaign. The moment before the maid's interruption, Olivia had been imagining Ramsay taking her into his arms. She tried to hide her excitement as she instructed the maid to show them in.

When the baron and Geordie appeared, Mayflower jumped off the sofa and hurried to the boy. "Mayflower!" said Geordie, stooping to pet the dog. He grinned up at Olivia. "Wolstan has been pining since she has left. She must come and visit him."

Olivia laughed. "You should have brought him."

Ramsay smiled. "The brute is not usually the most welcome of guests. Good afternoon, Lady Olivia. I hope we have not come at an inconvenient time."

"Certainly not." Olivia directed a mischievous look at him. "Of course, you did disturb my reading." She held up the book. "*The Age of Chivalry*, by Lord Ramsay." When he looked rather embarrassed, she continued. "I think it is a wonderful book, although I must not flatter you too much about it or you will become quite conceited.''

"Not Uncle," said Geordie earnestly. "He is very humble even though he is a genius.''

Olivia laughed and the baron glanced over at his nephew with a pained expression. "Geordie!''

"But it is what Professor Burry says,'' replied the boy.

"I am sure Lady Olivia knows that the professor may be a trifle prejudiced.''

"Indeed not, my lord,'' said Olivia. "I know he is the most objective of men. Now, do sit down, both of you.'' Geordie eagerly sat on the sofa next to Olivia while Ramsay took a seat in an armchair across from them. "How very handsome you look today, Geordie.''

The boy grinned. "It is my new clothes. Of course, this coat is not so grand as Sir Aubrey's. Uncle would not allow me to get a striped one like his.''

Olivia exchanged an amused glance with the baron. "Well, I assure you that coat is all the crack.'' Geordie looked very pleased with this remark, and Olivia continued. "I fear my cousin Aubrey and Lady Roxbury are not at home.''

The baron did not seem at all disappointed by this news. "They have gone out?''

"They are calling on Mr. Malvern.'' As Olivia expected, Ramsay frowned at the mention of the squire's name. "Aubrey was quite vexed with me for not going, but I have no desire to be introduced to every one of the squire's foxhounds.''

Geordie laughed and the baron smiled. "But I thought you liked hunting, Lady Olivia,'' said Ramsay.

"I like the excitement and the spectacle. I confess, like you, I do not enjoy the kill.''

"I like foxes," said Geordie, "and should hate to see one killed. You must promise not to tell Squire Malvern, Lady Olivia, but during the last hunt, I threw red herrings about to confuse the hounds.''

"Geordie," said the baron sternly.

"But, uncle," protested his nephew, "you said it was a capital thing to do."

Olivia burst into delighted laughter. "You are a rascal, Geordie, and I do not doubt that you inherited it from your uncle. I shall keep your secret, to guard you from the squire's rage."

"I am not afraid of him," said Geordie boldly.

"Then you are very brave," said Olivia, "for he terrifies me."

Geordie grinned. "You don't have to be afraid of him, for Uncle and I will protect you."

Olivia looked over at the baron. "I shall depend upon it." At that moment, Mayflower raised her sleek muzzle and regarded her mistress inquiringly. The dog leapt off the couch and paced across the room.

"I fear it is time for Mayflower's walk," said Olivia. At the word "walk" the dog's ears pricked up and she looked expectantly at her mistress. "Mayflower," said Olivia disapprovingly, "we have guests. We shall go out later."

"Poor Mayflower," said Geordie. "Could we not take her out now?"

"Perhaps we could do so, if that is acceptable to Lord Ramsay."

The baron smiled. "I should very much like that. The weather is quite good." Olivia excused herself and returned shortly, dressed in a walking outfit. She wore a modish pelisse of dove-gray kerseymere and a French bonnet trimmed with satin ribbons. She and her visitors left the house, followed by the excited whippet.

Once outside, Mayflower bounded off and a laughing Geordie ran after her. Olivia smiled as she watched the boy and the dog. "I fear Geordie will be very worn out trying to keep up with Mayflower."

"It is good for him to run," said Ramsay, who was also watching the boy. Olivia glanced at the baron, remembering how Burry had said he could not run like other boys as a child. It was fortunate that now his leg did not seem to bother him.

"Lady Olivia," said Ramsay, turning to meet her gaze. "I fear I was somewhat abrupt at our last meeting. You probably thought me rude."

"Lord Ramsay," said Olivia in mock surprise, "I did not think you cared if people thought you rude."

"I do not, generally speaking," returned his lordship, "but I do not want to be rude to you." The look in his dark eyes disconcerted Olivia.

"I know that you disapprove of hunting. I cannot expect you to approve of a hunt ball."

"But I could have been more gracious." He smiled again. "I do admit that I have had little practice at being gracious. I shall have to apologize to Roxbury, for I know that I have offended him."

"That would be good of you, my lord. My cousin is really not a bad fellow. I know that he is addicted to hunting and he is rather silly, but he is very good-hearted. Aubrey is like a brother to me and we have known each other from childhood. It is I who introduced him to Sophie. They are both my dearest friends." Ramsay made no remark and she continued, "I do wish you would reconsider going to the ball."

The baron shook his head. "No, I don't think so."

"I shan't press you." They walked on in silence for a time. Finally Olivia spoke. "Lord Ramsay, do you ever think that you would have liked to live in another time, the Middle Ages perhaps?"

He appeared amused by the question. "There are times when I think life then may have been superior in some ways to the modern age, but when I have my wits about me, I know very well it was a dreadful time in which to live. My ancestors spent far too much time defending Hawkesmuir from invading Scots. No, indeed, Lady Olivia,

I do not regret not having to take up my broadsword. But what of you? Are you content with these times?''

Olivia nodded. ''Very much so, although I confess that I would be very interested in meeting Robin Hood.''

Ramsay laughed and at that moment Geordie returned. ''Did you say Robin Hood, Lady Olivia?'' said the boy a bit breathlessly.

''Yes, Geordie. Your uncle and I were discussing him.''

''How I love the stories about him! They are Uncle's favorites too!''

Olivia laughed and looked over at the baron. ''Are they indeed, my lord?''

Ramsay grinned. ''I cannot deny it.''

''Then we have that in common.'' Olivia smiled. This remark made Geordie beg his uncle to tell a story about the hero of Sherwood Forest. After some coaxing by Olivia, the baron agreed and launched into a stirring account of Robin Hood's famous archery match, much to the delight of his two companions. At the conclusion of the tale, Olivia praised Ramsay's storytelling ability. She then smiled over at him. ''I'll wager, my lord, that you share Robin Hood's enthusiasm for the longbow.''

The baron reddened. ''Archery is a hobby of mine,'' he said.

Olivia laughed. ''I knew it!''

''And he is dashed good!'' exclaimed Geordie. ''I would think almost as good as Robin Hood! You must come to Hawkesmuir, Lady Olivia, and Uncle will demonstrate.''

''I will not,'' said Ramsay. ''Geordie, Lady Olivia has had enough of my demonstrating skills of medieval warfare.''

''But I have not!'' cried Olivia. ''You cannot disappoint me, my lord. I insist you shoot an apple off my head!''

The baron burst into laughter, but Geordie looked thoughtful. ''That would be a very good trick, uncle.''

''Then I shall shoot one off your head first, Geordie,'' said Ramsay.

Geordie grinned. "Perhaps a pumpkin, uncle."

The baron and Olivia laughed, and then they all proceeded back to the house. Olivia easily persuaded them to stay for tea.

Between bites of his bread and butter, Geordie smiled over at Olivia. "The professor has said there is to be a ball at Fenwyck. How I wish I were old enough to come."

"I do too, Geordie," said Olivia, "but it will not be long before you will be able to attend."

"I think it would be famous to go to a ball," said the boy. "Of course, I must learn how to dance first. Uncle says I shall have a dancing master in the spring."

"That is good, Geordie," said Olivia. "A gentleman must know how to dance. It is very important."

Geordie glanced over at his uncle and then back at Olivia. "But Uncle Gervas does not know how to dance."

"Geordie," said the baron, mortified at his nephew's words.

Olivia appeared surprised. "You do not know how to dance, my lord?"

He shrugged. "I never learned. When I was young, my leg prevented me from dancing. Now I have no desire to do so."

Ramsay's admission came as a revelation to Olivia. Could this be the reason for the baron's reluctance to attend the ball? "But you must learn to dance," she said.

"Why must I?" said the baron coolly.

Olivia hesitated. It had never occurred to her that someone would not want to dance. "Why, it is a most enjoyable pastime. I know you would enjoy it."

"I daresay I would not."

"You cannot know that if you have never tried it," persisted Olivia.

"And I shall never try it," replied Ramsay a trifle ill-humoredly.

"You are a provokingly stubborn man, Lord Ramsay, but I shall rise to the challenge. I shall teach you how to dance this very minute, and by my faith, you will enjoy it!''

The baron smiled. ''And if I don't enjoy it?''

''Then I promise to cease plaguing you about the subject.''

Geordie had listened to this exchange curiously. He looked questioningly at his uncle. The baron hesitated and then nodded. ''Very well, Lady Olivia, teach me how to dance, but I caution you, you may regret your fool-hardiness.''

Olivia smiled confidently. ''I do not think so.'' She turned to the boy. ''Geordie, can you play a waltz?''

Geordie nodded and eagerly hurried to the piano. He played a few bars and then looked over at Olivia. ''Is that all right?''

''Fine, but I think a trifle slower would better suit his lordship.'' Olivia rose from the sofa and Ramsay got up from his chair. He followed her to the open space in front of the fireplace. ''Take my hand,'' said Olivia, ''and put your other one here.'' She took his right hand and placed it around her waist. The baron, who had been quite skeptical about the undertaking, suddenly thought it would indeed be enjoyable. ''Now, follow me, my lord. I shall go very slowly. One, two, three, one, two, three.'' The baron appeared to have no trouble following this maneuver and Olivia called for Geordie to begin playing.

It did not take long for Ramsay to catch on to the step, although his leg prevented him from waltzing easily. However, with practice, he performed quite adequately and Olivia smiled at him. ''You are doing very well, Lord Ramay.''

''Nonsense, I would be laughed out of any London ballroom.''

''You would not. Indeed, I have danced with scores of gentlemen who cannot dance as well as you.''

The baron smiled slightly. ''I fear that is fustian, my lady. If you had the misfortune of dancing with me in town, you would quickly be wishing for a new partner.''

She fastened her blue eyes on his brown ones. "I would not, my lord." Her serious tone caught him off guard. He stopped dancing and the two of them stood regarding each other as if transfixed. Gazing down at her, Ramsay had the urge to pull her to him and cover her lips with passionate kisses. Momentarily forgetting Geordie's presence, the baron tightened his grip about her waist and leaned toward her.

However, at what was to the baron a most unfortunate moment, a man's voice boomed out. "Livy, Ramsay!" Startled, Olivia and the baron sprang apart. They turned to see Sir Aubrey and Sophie standing in the drawing room, eyeing them with keen interest. The music stopped abruptly and Geordie rose from the piano bench. "I must say I did not expect to find you dancing in the afternoon," said Aubrey disapprovingly.

Olivia tried to appear lighthearted, but she was still under the spell of the moment she and Ramsay had shared. "Geordie plays so beautifully that we could not resist."

Sophie, who had witnessed her friend in Ramsay's arms, smiled. "Yes, there are many times when I can hardly resist dancing." She turned to Geordie. "You do play very well, young man." She looked back at Ramsay. "How nice it is that you have come to call, Lord Ramsay. I see you have had tea. Why don't we all sit down and have a chat?"

Very much embarrassed by his lamentable lack of self-control, Ramsay frowned and, vowing to himself that he must be civil to the Roxburys, nodded and escorted Olivia back to the sofa.

16

"I daresay," said Sir Aubrey Roxbury as he dealt the cards, "I do not think playing whist with three people is quite the thing."

"I know, my dear," said Sophie, "but I fear we do not have a fourth. We will have to do the best we can."

The Roxburys and Olivia sat at the card table in the drawing room. A fire burned brightly in the fireplace and Mayflower lay curled up in front of it.

"Yes, Aubrey," said Olivia, smiling at her cousin, "there are worse things than playing whist with three people."

"That does not signify, Livy," returned the baronet as he finished dealing the cards. "It is most irregular. We will have to find another player for the future. I shall ask Malvern to join us next time."

"In that case," said Olivia, "you will still need a fourth, for I shall not play with that man."

Aubrey scowled. "Dash it, Livy, why are you so unreasonable where Malvern is concerned? I still think it was very bad of you not to have come with us today. Malvern was so very disappointed. The excuse that you had a headache sounded very lame."

"Oh, I did not think it seemed so very odd," commented Sophie, "but poor Mr Malvern was most unhappy that you did not accompany us. Indeed, it is clear he has a *tendre* for you."

"I'm sure he somehow managed to overcome his great disappointment," said Olivia, studying her cards. "You did say he was quite enthusiastic when he showed you his hounds."

"And with good reason," returned Aubrey. "I've never seen a finer pack. Most have Ranter's blood, you know. Malvern is clearly a man who knows dogs."

"And he is so very fond of them," said Sophie, "and the hounds adore him."

Olivia smiled. "I am glad that someone does."

" 'Pon my honor, cousin," said Aubrey irritably, "it is a puzzlement to me how you can prefer that bookish fellow Ramsay to a man like Malvern."

"I think Ramsay is rather handsome in a romantic sort of way," said Sophie. "Don't you find him so, Livy?"

"I do think he is handsome."

"It is obvious that you are enamored of him, Livy," said the baronet glumly. "You must take care, my girl. It was fortunate we came back when we did or I daresay the man would have taken the most shocking liberties."

Sophie laughed. "And I daresay that Livy was quite disappointed at our arrival."

"Sophie!" cried Aubrey with a horrified expression. When both of the ladies laughed, the baronet shook his head. "I thought the fellow was called 'Monk' Ramsay. That is certainly a misnomer. A gentleman who doesn't hunt cannot be trusted. I do not understand your fascination for a man who doesn't have the courage to take a jump or two."

"Lord Ramsay is an excellent horseman," said Olivia indignantly.

Aubrey raised his eyebrows. "I fear there is no hope in

talking sense to you. You are smitten with the man. Good God, I think it most peculiar that you can ignore the most dashing fellows in town falling at your feet and then become a silly moonling over Ramsay."

Olivia gave her cousin a warning look. "I think it best if we do not discuss this any further, Aubrey."

"Yes, yes," said Sophie, trying to smooth things over. "Come, let us concentrate on our cards."

The baronet made no reply, but looked peevishly at his cards, and the play began in a desultory fashion.

The following morning Olivia cantered across the moorland atop one of Aubrey's new hunters, a fine gray mare. She wore a claret-colored riding habit and high-crowned hat, its veil streaming after her in the chill wind. She was accompanied by Mayflower, who ran happily alongside the horse.

Although knowing that she was risking her cousin's displeasure in going out alone, Olivia felt a compelling need to get away from Fenwyck that morning. Since Sophie and Aubrey had not yet risen, she had no choice but to go by herself. In truth, she had been eager for the opportunity of solitary reflection.

As Olivia rode along, she thought of Ramsay. Remembering how they had danced and how she had stood looking into his dark eyes, she sighed. Aubrey was right. She was smitten with the baron. A slight smile came to Olivia's face as she thought about the first time she had seen him and the ridiculous wager that had caused them to meet.

Continuing on, Olivia directed her horse toward Ramsay's lands. She had not gone very far when a rider appeared on the horizon. Although Olivia could not see his face at such a distance, she knew that it was the baron. Ambling at his horse's side was the huge mastiff Wolstan.

Mayflower, catching sight of the other dog, raced excitedly toward him. Olivia's color rose and her pulse quickened as Ramsay galloped in her direction. She slowed her mare to a halt and watched the baron, riding with consummate skill astride a long-limbed bay horse, approach.

Ramsay smiled as he pulled his horse up beside her. He raised his beaver hat in greeting. "Lady Olivia."

"Lord Ramsay," said Olivia, feeling strangely shy in his presence. "Good morning."

"That is a fine-looking mare," he said, casting an admiring glance at the gray.

Olivia nodded, patting the animal's neck. "Yes, she is one of Aubrey's Irish hunters. But where is Destre? I expected to see you upon your charger."

"I have left both Destre and my lance at home," said the baron with a smile. "This is Sir Percival. I am trying him out and he is doing very nicely." Ramsay's spirited mount snorted and pawed the ground impatiently.

"I think your Sir Percival would like a run. Shall we race, my lord?"

"Very well." The baron looked across the moor. "To the church?"

Olivia espied the small village church in the distance. "Agreed." She smiled mischievously at him. "I fancy I shall beat you soundly, Lord Ramsay. Would you care to wager on it?"

"Wager?" returned his lordship, eyeing her curiously.

"If I win, you must attend the hunt ball, and if you win, I shall never mention it again."

"Those are high stakes indeed," said the baron with a slight smile.

"I thought it would appeal to your sporting blood."

Ramsay grinned. "I have no sporting blood, but since it is very clear that you do, I shall accept the wager."

"Good! Are you ready, my lord?"

The baron turned his horse and glanced over at her. "Ready."

Olivia nodded. "On the count of three. One . . . two . . . three!"

The horses sprang forward, their riders urging them ahead. They raced neck and neck across the moor and then Olivia's gray pulled ahead. The dogs had joined the race, Mayflower easily outdistancing all of them.

As Olivia galloped wildly onward, she glanced back and noted with satisfaction that Ramsay was now several lengths behind her. Shouting words of encouragement to her horse, Olivia continued on. The only obstacle between them and the church was a stone fence of moderate height. The gray mare took it easily and then Ramsay's bay sailed over it.

Now in the final stretch of the race, the horses thundered toward their goal. Ramsay gave the bay its head. The thoroughbred, a worthy example of his breed, surged forward, soon overtaking Olivia and leaving her behind. Olivia vainly tried to regain the lead, but despite her gray mare's gallant effort, Ramsay reached the finish well ahead of her.

They both pulled their horses up near the churchyard. "So you have won, my lord," said Olivia rather breathlessly. "I am undone by superior horsemanship."

"You are undone by a superior horse, ma'am. Your horsemanship is not in question. You are superb."

Olivia blushed. "Such a compliment is consolation to my loss. But you are the victor and you do not have to go to the ball."

Ramsay smiled. "I confess that I am not displeased by the result."

"I shall abide by the wager and not pester you about going, but I am very disappointed that you will not be there."

"So you were so eager to show your abilities as a dancing master, Lady Olivia?"

Olivia nodded. "Indeed so, and I very much regret not having the opportunity. I am sure, Lord Ramsay, that you are relieved at not having to endure dancing with me again.''

''My dear lady, if I knew that attending the ball just meant dancing with you, no one could keep me from it.''

This unsettling remark made Olivia blush again. However, before she could reply, two more riders approached. Ramsay would have thought any interruption at that moment most untimely, but noting the identity of the intruders, he cursed to himself. It was Squire Malvern. Accompanying him was a lady of Amazonian proportions, who smiled good-naturedly at them.

Olivia immediately saw a resemblance between the woman and Malvern and suspected that this was his sister. Malvern confirmed her suspicions by making the introduction. ''Lady Olivia,'' he said, smiling at her and pointedly ignoring Ramsay. ''May I present my sister, Lady Horsley? Caroline, this is Lady Olivia Dunbar.'' He paused and then added with seeming reluctance, ''And you know Ramsay, of course.''

''Certainly,'' said Lady Horsley, speaking in a loud voice. ''How do you do, Lady Olivia? Roger has told me so much about you, and you are certainly as pretty as he said. And by heaven, you can sit a horse! I saw the two of you riding, and the jump was well done indeed. And, Ramsay, that is a fine bit of blood and bone beneath you. Why, he took the fence as if it were nothing.''

Malvern, who did not like the admiring tone of his sister's words, frowned at the baron. ''It was not much of a fence. Why, an infant on a pony could have taken it with ease.''

Olivia eyed the squire with disfavor. ''I daresay taking such an obstacle is hardly a great accomplishment, yet it was a jump of respectable height.''

''Aye, it was,'' said Lady Horsley. ''Don't be absurd, Roger.'' She glanced down at the dogs and smiled broadly. ''Fine-looking dogs. Are they yours, Ramsay?''

"The mastiff is mine, but the whippet belongs to Lady Olivia."

"A lovely little hound, Lady Olivia," said Caroline. "I should like a whippet. Coursing rabbits would be such fun, and they are such pretty dogs." She looked over at her brother. "Don't you think a whippet would look well with Clarence's pug?"

Malvern shook his head distastefully. "Clarence's pug? That yapping monkey! Hardly a dog for a man."

"Don't be horrid, Roger. Loki is the sweetest creature imaginable." Lady Horsely turned to Olivia and Ramsay. "I fear my brother only likes foxhounds. I confess a fondness for them myself, but then I do love nothing better than the hunt. You cannot know how glad I was to hear that you hunt, Lady Olivia. I have been the only lady riding to the hounds for far too long. What a glorious sport it is! I can scarcely wait until the first hunt. Thank goodness, it is less than a week away. I am sure you are looking forward to it as much as I am, Lady Olivia."

Olivia nodded. "Yes," she said, glancing over at Ramsay to see his reaction. As expected, he did not look very pleased.

"I am not one to brag," said Lady Horsely, "but our hunt is among the best in the kingdom. There is no country better suited for hunting than Northumberland, and my brother's pack is unequaled anywhere."

At this remark Malvern grinned at his sister. "No other hounds can hold a candle to them," he said with almost paternal pride.

"My cousin Aubrey is very impressed with them," commented Olivia.

"Your cousin seems to be an admirable man," said Lady Horsley. "It was very good of him to host the hunt ball. I would have been quite daunted at the prospect of giving such an entertainment at such short notice. Although I myself do not like balls overmuch, I know that many would have been sorely disappointed if there was not going to be one. Oh, yes, everyone will be there.''

Malvern looked over at Ramsay. "Not everyone, Caroline," he said. "I'm sure his lordship will not favor the Roxburys with his presence."

The baron made no reply, but directed an icy look at the squire.

"But you should go, Ramsay," said Lady Horsley. "There are always too many ladies without dancing partners."

"That is something Lady Olivia will not have to worry about," said the squire. "Every gentleman in the county will want to dance with her. However, I insist you allow me the most dances."

Looking at Malvern's grinning face, Olivia found herself suddenly dreading the ball. "A lady cannot make any promises, Mr. Malvern."

"Indeed not," said Lady Horsley, "but do agree to dance with my brother at least once, Lady Olivia, or he will be even less fit to live with than he usually is." The squire's sister directed an affectionate look at him and then turned to Olivia. "In which direction are you riding? We shall accompany you."

Olivia looked over at the baron and found his expression quite grim. "I must return to Fenwyck," she said. "Why don't you all accompany me?"

"A splendid idea," replied Lady Horsley enthusiastically.

Olivia looked again at Ramsay. "Will you come, my lord?"

He shook his head. "You must excuse me, Lady Olivia. I am expected back at Hawkesmuir." Then, after nodding coolly to Malvern and tipping his hat to the ladies, the baron rode off, followed by his mastiff, Wolstan.

"I have always thought Ramsay a peculiar man," said Lady Horsley, watching his retreating figure, "but I did not realize he was a horseman. He has a very good seat and seems an excellent judge of horseflesh to be so mounted. Perhaps I have misjudged him.''

"You are easily impressed, Caroline. I cannot believe he is much of a horseman. After all, he doesn't hunt.'' Malvern's tone implied that this was the greatest of eccentricities.

"It is not Lord Ramsay's horsemanship that prevents him from hunting,'' said Olivia. "He disapproves of the sport.''

"And that is much worse,'' said the squire. "What sort of English gentleman would disapprove of hunting?''

Lady Horsley looked puzzled. "But why ever would Ramsay disapprove of hunting?'' she asked Olivia.

"He does not think it sporting,'' replied Olivia. "His sympathies lie with the fox.''

"Bah,'' retorted Lady Horsley. "A fox is more than a match for the hunt.''

"Not according to Ramsay, I'm sure,'' said the squire contemptuously. "When he was a boy, he couldn't even bear to see a rabbit killed. How we laughed at him! I daresay he is the sort of fool who is crying to Parliament to outlaw dogfighting!''

"Why, I think it should be outlawed,'' said Olivia indignantly. "It is cruel and barbarous.''

Although dogfighting was the squire's favorite amusement save for hunting, he thought it wise to humor Olivia. "Perhaps there is something to be said against it,'' he said.

"Then you must cease betting on the village matches, Roger,'' said Lady Horsley, grinning at her brother.

Malvern scowled at her, but then smiled at Olivia. "Shall we be off to Fenwyck?'' he said, hoping to turn Olivia's attention away from dogfighting.

Olivia nodded, and after directing one more glance at the baron's retreating form, she turned her horse and rode off with the squire and his sister.

*   *   *

The baron returned from his ride in an ill humor. He went into the library and found Professor Burry perusing the bookshelves. "So you are back, Ramsay," said the professor, looking over his spectacles at his lordship.

Ramsay nodded, but said nothing. Burry eyed his young friend curiously. "You appear to be in a black mood, my boy."

"Perhaps so. I met Lady Olivia on my ride."

"I would not have thought that would have put you in a bad temper."

The baron smiled slightly. "No, but then we met Malvern and his sister. They talked of hunting and that deuced ball." He seemed to want to change the subject. "Where is Geordie?"

"He is in the schoolroom writing an essay on Marcus Aurelius. It should keep him busy for some time."

Ramsay smiled again and went to his desk, where he sat down and began to leaf through some papers on it. The professor continued to browse among the books for a time, and then, taking one from the shelf, he went over to where the baron was sitting.

"I daresay it was quite fortunate, your meeting Lady Olivia this morning," said Burry. "Such a charming young woman. One cannot help liking her." He looked closely at Ramsay. "I suspect you are very fond of her."

The baron looked up from his notes and met the professor's inquisitive gaze. "Dash it all, sir, of course I'm fond of her."

"Why, that is marvelous! Why the glum face, then?"

Ramsay shook his head. "I think it prudent that I put aside my feelings for the lady. We are so very different. She would be happier with a man who shares her love of hunting and society."

"You mean like Malvern?" The baron scowled and the professor grinned again. "Really, my lad, for such a clever fellow, you are being quite a dunce. It is obvious that Lady Olivia has affection for you."

"Come, Professor," replied Ramsay, "that is absurd."

"It is not in the least absurd. I think you are a fool if you allow that young lady to get away. Why don't you attend Ramsay's ball?"

"You know how much I detest such things."

"That does not signify. You should go. Dress up in your new clothes and you will look like a proper buck."

Ramsay laughed. "I shall look like the eccentric baron in new evening clothes. That is all."

"You will look splendid." Burry regarded him seriously. "Truly, my boy, I think you should go to the ball."

Ramsay frowned. "I shall consider it," he said.

The professor, pleased with the reply, began to talk of other subjects.

17

The scene outside Malvern Hall typified English country life. Gathered about the grounds of the Tudor manor were horsemen, most of them dressed in scarlet coats with the distinctive buttons of the Malvern Hunt. The gentlemen in their beaver hats, doeskin breeches, and shiny top boots looked dashing atop their hunters.

The foxhounds of the squire's pack wandered about the riders, their noses twitching with excitement. In addition to the dogs and horsemen, there was a crowd of onlookers, mostly ladies who stood admiring the gentlemen. There were also a number of curious villagers who had come to observe the upper class at its pastime.

The spectators were very much interested to find another lady in the hunting party. They were well accustomed to the sight of Lady Horsley dressed in her scarlet riding habit. Long the only female in attendance, she had ridden since girlhood and was among the most fearless of riders.

Olivia's presence sparked much comment. She looked splendid in a close-fitting sky-blue riding habit, perched atop Aubrey's spirited gray mare. Her golden curls were visible beneath a high-crowned hat of matching blue. Although most of the ladies in attendance thought it rather

154

unseemly for a female to join the gentlemen in the hunt, they could not help but be envious of the striking picture Olivia presented.

Olivia glanced about the crowd, noting the number of fine-looking horses. There was an air of excitement among the riders, and although Olivia could not help but feel it, she found she was viewing the hunt with less enthusiasm than might be expected. She kept thinking of Ramsay and imagining his displeasure. His good opinion meant so much to her that she wondered if she should be participating in the hunt.

"Lady Olivia!" Lady Horsley's stentorian voice brought Olivia out of her reverie.

"Lady Horsley." Olivia smiled at Malvern's sister and noted the gentleman riding beside her with some interest. So this was the Sir Clarence that the squire so disdained, thought Olivia. He was a portly man of middle years with a round, jolly face.

"I must present my husband to you. Lady Olivia, this is Sir Clarence Horsley. Clarence, Lady Olivia."

"Your servant, ma'am," said Sir Clarence, tipping his beaver hat and smiling brightly at Olivia. "My brother-in-law has spoken so highly of you. My dear Caroline is so pleased at having another lady in the hunt."

"Indeed I am," replied Lady Horsley, looking toward the spectators. "Those simpering females fear either the hard riding or society's opinion too much to hunt."

"But do not forget, my dear," said Sir Clarence, "that few ladies can ride like you." He grinned over at Olivia. "Few gentlemen either."

Lady Horsley smiled fondly at her husband. "That may be true," she conceded, "but then, there has never been a Malvern who could not ride."

"Nor a Horsley that could," added Sir Clarence.

Caroline laughed loudly at this remark. "But you do try, don't you, dearest?" she said.

Her husband grinned again and looked over at Olivia. "Have you hunted very much, Lady Olivia?"

"Some," replied Olivia. "Mostly with my father's pack in Surrey."

"Well, you'll not be disappointed with our hunt," said Lady Horsley.

"I am certain of that," said Olivia. "The Malvern Hunt is known throughout England."

Caroline smiled proudly. "Aye, you will see good sport this day, Lady Olivia. And where is your cousin?"

"He is there near your brother." Olivia nodded in the direction of Malvern and Aubrey. "My cousin is always one to hang about the master, and I fear he is sometimes judged a nuisance." Olivia watched Malvern and noted that the squire seemed intent upon his duties as master of the hunt. At present he was engaged in a serious discussion with his huntsman, who was easily identified by the horn he traditionally carried. Olivia was glad that the squire was so preoccupied with his responsibilities, for they kept him well away from her.

However, after concluding his words with his huntsman, Malvern glanced in Olivia's direction and then rode over to her, Aubrey following behind. "Roger," said Caroline, smiling broadly at her brother. "The hounds are in fine fettle. There is old Jackanapes looking like a pup." She pointed to one of the dogs and turned to explain to Olivia. "He is Roger's favorite."

"Aye, he is a rare one," said the squire, glancing from the hound to Olivia. "And so are you, Lady Olivia. By God, you look splendid."

Olivia acknowledged the compliment with a polite but reserved nod. "It appears to be a fine day for a hunt, Mr. Malvern."

"That it is, but then, any day is a fine day for a hunt, by my way of thinking." He smiled again at Olivia and she felt somewhat uncomfortable at his gaze. "I do fear that I cannot tarry here. We are off soon. Let up hope we have good sport today." The squire tipped his hat to Olivia and rode off.

"I daresay, Lady Horsley," said Aubrey, watching the squire with admiration, "your brother is the finest master in England. What good fortune my buying Fenwyck. Oh, it appears we are moving out."

The hounds, Malvern, and his associates started off, and the others turned their horses to follow. As she walked her horse along with the rest of the riders, Olivia found herself once again thinking of Ramsay. She wondered what he would be doing at that moment, and despite her old love of hunting, she wished that she were with him.

Baron Ramsay rode slowly across the moor, accompanied by his nephew, Geordie. Sir Percival seemed impatient with the slow pace, but the baron held him in check so that Geordie's pony could keep up. The boy could not fail to note that his uncle seemed unusually abstracted that morning. Ramsay said little and, indeed, seemed almost unaware of his nephew's presence.

"Could we not run a bit, uncle?" said Geordie. "Poor Sir Percival does not like to walk, and Queen Mab would like a good gallop." The boy patted his fat black pony affectionately. "Let us race to the top of the hill."

"If you wish," said Ramsay. "I shall give you a head start."

Geordie needed no further urging, but kicked his pony's sides and rode off. After allowing the boy to get a good distance away, the baron followed. Although keeping the thoroughbred from his full speed, Ramsay easily caught up to the pony and, passing Geordie, soon arrived at the top of the hill. There he pulled the stallion to a halt and waited for his nephew to join him.

Geordie grinned as he drew alongside his uncle. "Poor Mab feels like a tortoise beside Percival. It is folly to race you." He patted the pony again and looked out at the surrounding countryside visible from their vantage point on the high ground. "Did you hear that, uncle?" The notes of the huntsman's horn penetrated the crisp November air.

Ramsay frowned. "The Malvern Hunt."

"They have sighted the fox," said Geordie. "I do hope he gets away. If only I had put some red herrings about."

"You'll get into trouble that way, my boy. It is best for you to keep well away from it."

The horn sounded again. "He has probably gone to Farmer Bailey's covert," said Geordie. "The hounds will try to draw him out."

Ramsay looked toward the woods that he knew obscured the covert. He detected flashes of red beyond the trees, and although he was tempted to ride off, the knowledge that Olivia was among the hunters made him stay.

"The fox!" cried Geordie. The small red animal made a wild dash across the open country. "He's getting away!" However, the loud howls of the hounds announced that the fox's attempt at escape had not gone unnoticed. A moment later the pack came into view, followed by Malvern and the huntsmen.

The baron frowned again as he caught sight of Malvern and then looked to see the other riders. He quickly spotted Olivia, a blue figure among the army of scarlet-coated sportsmen.

"It is Lady Olivia!" cried Geordie.

Ramsay did not reply, but kept his eyes riveted upon Olivia. She was among the main body of riders, keeping up with the best of them. They came to a ditch and he watched her take it with ease. Then, coming to another obstacle, a tall stone fence, Olivia's horse took the jump, but then, to Ramsay's horror, the animal stumbled and fell, throwing Olivia to the ground.

"Oh no!" cried Geordie.

Without a word the baron spurred his horse and tore down the hill. He rode recklessly across the rugged terrain, urging his horse onward despite the fact that he was separated from the hunt by a wide and treacherous ravine. Seemingly oblivious of the danger, Ramsay hurtled across it. Sir Percival landed neatly on the other side and raced ahead. When in a few moments Ramsay reached Olivia, he jumped from the horse and ran to her.

Some of the other riders had stopped and Sir Aubrey and Sir Clarence Horsley had dismounted. Aubrey was bending over a somewhat disoriented Olivia. Brusquely pushing Sir Clarence aside, Ramsay knelt down beside her. "Olivia, are you hurt!"

Olivia regarded him in some confusion. "Lord Ramsay? What are you doing here?"

"That does not signify. Are you hurt?"

She shook her head. "Only a trifle shaken and very much embarrassed. I think I can stand. Would one of you gentlemen please help me up?"

Sir Aubrey was rather irked when the baron quickly lifted Olivia to her feet, for he much preferred to help his cousin himself. Ramsay ignored Aubrey completely and viewed Olivia with concern. "It looked like a bad fall," he said, continuing to hold her. "Are you sure you were not injured?"

She smiled up at him. "I assure you I am all right." Olivia tried to sound confident, but still feeling rather unsteady, she was glad of the support of his strong arms. "But what of my horse?"

Aubrey had turned to the gray mare and was examining its legs. "No harm done," he said. "Thank God for that."

The baron scowled at Aubrey. "You show more concern for your horse than your cousin, Roxbury."

Aubrey's face grew red and he replied indignantly, "Dammit, Ramsay, that is only because you will not allow me to get near her. There is no need for you to be here. We can take care of Olivia very well ourselves."

"Oh, yes, you take very good care of her," muttered

the baron, "allowing her to ride with a bunch of hunting-mad idiots. She might have been killed."

Olivia pulled away from Ramsay and appeared very much insulted. "Really, sir, how dare you speak so to my cousin? And Aubrey does not *allow* me to do anything. I am my own mistress. You must just consider me one of the hunting-mad idiots."

The baron frowned. "I did not mean—"

"It is very clear what you meant."

"You cannot blame me for thinking it foolhardy for a lady to ride like some sort of wild Mongol."

"By heaven, Ramsay," said Sir Clarence, entering the conversation, "the only one I saw riding like a wild Mongol was you. Good God, I could scarcely believe the jump you took. I daresay no one else would have dared attempt it. Not even Roger Malvern."

"I think you had better leave, Ramsay," said Aubrey. "You are not needed here."

The baron turned to Olivia, and since that lady was still irritated at his remarks, she frowned and did not meet his gaze. "Very well," he said curtly. He went to his horse and quickly mounted Sir Percival. Then, without another word, he rode off.

"The audacity of the man," fumed Aubrey.

"Indeed," said Sir Clarence, watching the baron urge his horse into a gallop, "but the fellow certainly can ride."

"Aye," said one of the other riders still mounted nearby. "I cannot believe he made that jump. Good God, he's trying it again!"

They all turned and watched as Ramsay approached the wide ravine. Olivia's eyes widened in alarm. She had ridden that way before and was well aware of the distance from one side to the other. Under Ramsay's expert hands, the stallion vaulted across without any difficulty.

"By Jupiter!" cried Sir Clarence. "I've never seen the like of it." The other gentlemen who had witnessed Ramsay's feat voiced similar sentiments and marveled at the baron's daring. Olivia, although not as surprised as the others at Ramsay's horsemanship, was nonetheless impressed. However, she was less concerned with his equestrian skill than with the words they had just exchanged.

"Do you wish to go back, Olivia?" said Aubrey.

Olivia shook her head. "No, I shall continue. And I have kept you gentlemen too long. Do go on." The other riders did so, and she, Aubrey, and Clarence returned to their horses. They then started after the distant hunting field.

18

Those who had participated in the Malvern Hunt that day had found it rather disappointing. The fox had gone to ground, and despite the best efforts of a terrier brought along for such a possibility, it had got away.

Squire Malvern was especially displeased by the day's activities, for not only had they failed to obtain a kill, but he was treated numerous times to the story of Lord Ramsay's remarkable jump. Since the squire had not witnessed it, he dismissed it as fustian. Still, it bothered Malvern that Ramsay had become the object of admiration. However, there was some comfort in hearing that Lady Olivia had been very vexed with the baron, and Malvern was certain that the hunt ball would be a perfect opportunity to engage that lady's affections.

Unlike the squire, Olivia was not looking forward to the ball. That evening as she sat in her dressing room while her maid put the finishing touches on her coiffure, Olivia frowned. Since returning to Fenwyck, she had thought constantly of the baron. Why was he so unreasonable, she asked herself. It was one thing for Ramsay to have opinions against hunting, but quite another for him to express himself in such an insulting manner.

"I'm finished, m'lady," said the maid.

"Oh, thank you," said Olivia, glancing absently at her reflection in the mirror. As usual, Olivia looked exquisite. Her ball dress was fashioned from rose-colored satin topped with an overdress of white lace. The high-waisted bodice and tiny puff sleeves were trimmed with pearls. Around Olivia's neck was a double strand of pearls and in her blond hair were satin flowers.

Rising from her dressing table, Olivia took her gloves and fan from the maid and went to find Sophie. Lady Roxbury was nearly ready. Her maid was fastening an emerald necklace about her throat just as Olivia entered the room. "Thank goodness you are here, Livy. I am not at all sure if this necklace is quite the thing."

"Why ever not? It is lovely. Indeed, you look stunning. The green of your gown suits you splendidly."

Lady Roxbury looked dubiously into the mirror. "It will have to do, I suppose."

"Good heavens, Sophie! You are nervous! I have never seen you like this. Why, in town you have presided over much grander functions than this!"

"Oh, I know that, but I am acquainted with so few of my guests, and it is so important to Aubrey that the ball go well."

"And why is that? I thought Aubrey considered it so provincial here."

"He does, but that does not signify in the least. I have never seen him so happy. Of course, that is the Malvern Hunt's doing. He had such a wonderful time today." Sophie paused and then continued. "Except, of course, for the unfortunate meeting with Lord Ramsay."

Olivia frowned. "I do not know how the baron came to be there. It was so embarrassing having him see my fall. And then he called us hunting-mad idiots."

Sophie laughed. "He is a perceptive man, your baron."

"Oh, Sophie," said Olivia, smiling at her friend.

"Well, I think it was very romantic that he came rush-

ing down to help you. The way Sir Clarence Horsley told
it, it must have been very exciting. Even Aubrey admits
Ramsay is quite a horseman. I daresay the topic will be on
everyone's tongue at the ball tonight. It is a pity that
Ramsay will not be there.'' Sophie eyed Olivia, interested
in her friend's reaction to this remark.

Olivia frowned again. ''I am sure that it is for the best
that Lord Ramsay does not attend.''

''Fiddle! You know you wish he would come.'' When
her friend did not deny it, Sophie smiled and then rose from
her chair. ''We cannot dawdle any longer. The guests will
be arriving.''

Olivia nodded and halfheartedly followed Sophie from
the room.

The lighthearted country-dance music was ill-suited to
Olivia's mood. She smiled and tried to look cheerful as
she took the hand of the young man to her right, but after a
quick turn with that gentleman, she was handed back to
Malvern.

The squire was having a marvelous time. Despite Olivia's attempts to avoid him, Malvern had managed to plague
her throughout the evening. He was in a boisterously good
humor, having downed a number of glasses of punch, and
when they danced, he acted as though he and Olivia were
on the most intimate of terms.

It took all of Olivia's self-control to refrain from giving
the squire a rude setdown. However, knowing how important the ball was to Sophie and Aubrey, she did not want
to make a scene. Olivia therefore endured Malvern's attentions as well as she could.

When the music stopped, all the ladies and gentlemen
bowed and curtsied to each other. The squire grinned at
her. ''The old dances are best. They've life in them. I
much prefer them to newfangled waltzes.''

Olivia felt hopeful. ''Then surely you will not want to
dance any waltzes, Mr. Malvern.''

The squire winked at her. "I don't care what I dance as long as it's with you, Olivia."

Olivia tried to disguise her loathing for the man. If she could only rid herself of his bothersome attentions, she thought as she took his arm and allowed him to escort her from the dancing area. Malvern led her back to Aubrey and greeted her cousin jovially. "Roxbury, there has never been such a splendid ball. You are to be congratulated."

Sir Aubrey smiled. "You are to be congratulated on your choice of a dancing partner." Ignoring the look Olivia gave him, the baronet continued. "It is a bang-up affair."

"Aye," said the squire, "and everyone is grateful to you and Lady Roxbury."

Aubrey smiled at Malvern's remark. However, he would have been far less pleased had he known what the squire was actually thinking about him. Although Malvern could not fault his host on the ball, the squire had only contempt for Aubrey's dandified clothes. Indeed, at the punch bowl, Malvern had remarked to his friends that he considered Roxbury a coxcomb.

Olivia fanned herself and looked about the room, hoping that another gentleman would join them. Yet, although a number of young men glanced in Olivia's direction, they were reluctant to approach, since they feared risking the squire's displeasure. "Might I ask you to get me a glass of punch, Mr. Malvern?" said Olivia.

The squire was most eager to comply with this request and hurried off. When he had gone, Sir Aubrey looked over at his cousin. "I am glad to see that you and Malvern are getting along so well this evening."

"Oh, Aubrey, I can barely tolerate the man. I have never had such a dreadful night. Malvern had latched on to me like a leech and I find his attentions odious." Noting her cousin's pained expression, Olivia smiled. "Don't worry, Aubrey, I shall be polite to him."

"I had hoped you might appreciate Malvern after seeing how rude Ramsay was today."

"Whatever I might think of the baron, it does not change my opinion of Mr. Malvern. Oh dear, here he comes."

Having fulfilled his mission with alacrity, the squire presented Olivia with a glass of punch. She thanked him dutifully and drank it slowly. This allowed Malvern and Aubrey time to discuss the squire's hounds, and Olivia thought she might scream if she heard the words "Ranter's blood" said once more.

"You must allow me the next dance, Olivia," said Malvern.

Olivia hesitated and considered telling him that she would rather rest. Then, deciding that it was preferable to dance with him than to sit in a chair enduring his conversation, she nodded. The squire grinned again and offered her his arm.

Although Olivia dearly loved to waltz, she was none too pleased to find that was the next dance. Like the squire, she would have rather had another country dance, since it involved changing partners with frequency.

The music had barely begun when Olivia glanced over at the main entrance to the ballroom. A look of astonishment came to her face and she missed a step, causing her to bump against Malvern. There stood Lord Ramsay dressed in his black evening clothes, surveying the company.

The squire, rather surprised at the lapse in Olivia's usual dancing skill, looked out in the direction of her gaze. Seeing the baron, he frowned darkly. Olivia quickly recovered and danced flawlessly, but Malvern could not fail to note that her eyes seemed glued to the figure of Ramsay. The squire was startled and irritated to see the baron dressed in modish evening clothes that fitted his trim frame splendidly. Looking down at Olivia, Malvern silently cursed Ramsay and his fine London clothes.

The baron looked out into the crowded ballroom and

found himself wondering whether he should have come. He detested balls, and the fact that this one celebrated the start of the hunting season made it even more anomalous that he should be there.

Indeed, Ramsay had decided only at the last moment to attend. Yet, having regretted his words with Olivia that morning, the baron wanted very much to see her and make things right. Therefore he was even willing to endure the ball.

Ramsay searched the assembly for Olivia, and after finally spotting her, he frowned. There she was waltzing in the arms of Squire Malvern. Feelings of jealousy and resentment welled up in him and he suddenly realized that he had been a fool to come. He was ready to turn and leave when a feminine voice called out to him. "Lord Ramsay, how wonderful that you are here."

Retreat now impossible, his lordship managed to smile at Sophie Roxbury. "I fear I am very late."

"It is a happy surprise to see you, sir." Sophie took the baron's arm and led him into the ballroom. "It is such a crush of people. I am sure you know most everyone."

Ramsay shook his head. "No, many are unknown to me. It has been some time since I have attended a social function."

She smiled up at him. "Well, I am very honored that you have chosen to attend our ball. Oh, here comes the vicar. He is such a dear man and appears most eager to see you."

Ramsay smiled in return. "I daresay he is. The church needs a new bell tower."

Sophie laughed, but had no time to reply, for the vicar, his wife, and a young gentleman appeared before them. "Lord Ramsay," said the clergyman enthusiastically, "what a privilege to meet you here. I am sure you know Mrs. Penworthy." The vicar's wife, a stout amiable-looking woman, bobbed a curtsy and Ramsay bowed politely. "I do not think you have met my curate, Mr. Simms. Simms, this is Lord Ramsay.''

Mr. Simms, a tall lanky young man with wispy straw-colored hair and sharp features, bowed to the baron and seemed quite thrilled when Ramsay extended his hand to him. "This is a very great honor, my lord," said the young man, shaking the baron's hand. "I have heard so much about you.''

Ramsay raised a dark eyebrow. "Indeed?''

"Oh, yes, Professor Wakefield at Cambridge speaks very highly of you, my lord.''

"Wakefield? Oh, yes, I have corresponded with him.''

"And I have read your book," continued Mr. Simms eagerly. "If I may say so, it is dashed good.''

"You are very kind, Mr. Simms," replied Ramsay, rather amused at the young man.

Emboldened by the baron's civility, the curate continued. "I should very much like to discuss your lordship's views on the conflict between the church and secular authorities in the time of Henry the Second.''

Sophie smiled at the young man. "I am sure, Mr. Simms, that that is a fascinating topic, but hardly a subject for a ball.''

When the curate looked rather crestfallen, Ramsay eyed him sympathetically. "Lady Roxbury is right, Mr. Simms, but do call on me at Hawkesmuir Castle and we will discuss the matter. I'm sure Professor Burry would like to talk with you as well. Yes, call on me whenever your duties will allow it.''

Simms appeared overwhelmed at Lord Ramsay's words. From what he had heard about Ramsay, the curate had not expected such an invitation. He somehow managed to murmur that he would be honored to accept his lordship's kind offer.

Ramsay then turned to the vicar. "I have heard that the church needs a new bell tower, sir. You may count upon me for assistance.''

The Reverend Mr. Penworthy was quite delighted at this and thanked the baron heartily. After exchanging a few more words with them, the vicar and his party took their leave.

As he watched them go, Ramsay wondered at what had come over him. Had he really invited the gawky young Mr. Simms to Hawkesmuir Castle? He smiled to himself, glad that he had done so.

"You certainly have made yourself popular with the clergy, Lord Ramsay," said Sophie, eyeing him with some amusement.

"I am glad I am popular with someone."

Sophie directed a knowing look at him. "You are very popular with someone else, my lord," she said. She laughed at his look of embarrassment. "You know that I am speaking of Olivia."

"I do not know that she will be so eager to see me. She is occupied with Malvern."

"My dear Lord Ramsay, Livy detests that man. She will be very grateful to you if you would rescue her from him." The baron looked toward the dancers as the orchestra played the last strains of the waltz, and he watched as Malvern escorted Olivia from the dance floor. "Come, my lord," said Sophie, taking the baron's arm and leading him away.

The squire returned Olivia once again to her cousin and was not happy to see that Aubrey had now been joined by Sophie and Lord Ramsay. Lady Roxbury smiled merrily at him. "What great good fortune that his lordship decided to attend," she said.

The baron nodded coolly to Malvern and bowed to Olivia. "Good evening, Lady Olivia."

"How nice to see you, Lord Ramsay," said Olivia, all her former irritation with him completely vanished.

"The baron has just met the vicar's curate," said Sophie. "Mr. Simms has read his book and Lord Ramsay has been so kind as to invite him to Hawkesmuir to discuss something or other. I can't remember what, but I'm sure it is a most fascinating topic.''

"Simms," said Malvern contemptuously, "that namby-pamby fellow? He's a timid boy who hides behind his books.''

Ramsay's expression grew ominous and Sophie hastened in. "Oh, I think he is a nice young man. And Lord Ramsay is going to contribute to the church's bell tower. Shouldn't we do so too, Aubrey?''

The baronet nodded. "As you wish, my dear.''

Olivia smiled at the squire. "Surely, Mr. Malvern, you will also want to make a donation.''

Although it was clearly not his intention, the squire nodded. "Of course,'' he said.

"I shall tell the vicar at first opportunity that he has two more contributors," said Sophie. "He will be so very pleased.''

Olivia nearly laughed at Malvern's expression. Noting the approach of Sir Clarence and Lady Horsley, Olivia smiled. "Mr. Malvern, here are your sister and Sir Clarence.''

The squire viewed his brother-in-law with the same lack of enthusiasm he had had for his contribution to the bell tower. He frowned at Sir Clarence, but that gentleman merely grinned at Malvern and the others. "Ramsay," he said affably, "everyone is talking about you.''

"I shouldn't wonder at that," muttered the squire.

"They are talking about Ramsay's jump," said Lady Horsley, eyeing her brother with disfavor. "How I wish I might have seen it. To have jumped that ravine is remarkable, but to have jumped it twice is utterly astonishing.''

"It was something to see," said Aubrey with grudging admiration.

Malvern was irked to hear the baron praised. "It must have been a very good horse.''

"It was a good horse," said Olivia, smiling at Ramsay, "but an even better horseman.''

"Aye," said Caroline, nodding, "that is what I have heard. What a pity that you do not hunt, Ramsay, but if you change your mind, you would be very welcome in the Malvern Hunt."

"I think the master of the hunt should have something to say about that, Caroline," said the squire.

"Don't worry, Malvern," returned Ramsay. "I have no intention of wishing to join you."

"Indeed not," said Olivia, casting a mischievous look at the baron. "His lordship is not a hunting-mad Mongol, after all."

Ramsay smiled at her. "Lady Olivia, would you do me the honor of allowing me this dance?"

"I should be very happy to," returned Olivia, taking his arm. After nodding to the others, the baron escorted her away.

"I am surprised that you are speaking to me," said Ramsay.

"And I am surprised that you came. After all, you did win the race and therefore you were not obliged to come."

He smiled. "But how else could I demonstrate my newfound dancing ability? I am hopeful it will be a waltz. I would certainly make a muddle of anything else."

"I am sure it will be a waltz, but if not, we can retreat."

"I am glad of that," said the baron. He then regarded her with a serious expression. "I am sorry that I angered you this morning. You must believe that I would never wish to offend you."

"I know," she said. "I think I just felt very foolish. Of course, I must say I did not like to think of myself as one of Genghis Khan's troops."

Ramsay smiled again. "There is no danger of your being taken for one. You look beautiful."

Olivia blushed. "I am not accustomed to such flummery from you, my lord."

"It is only the truth, Olivia."

Surprised and pleased at the baron omitting her title, she smiled. "I am so glad you've come, Lord Ramsay."

"Perhaps you might reserve that comment until after we dance." He paused. "Do you think you could call me Gervas?"

"Gladly . . . Gervas."

The baron grinned and the orchestra began to play. "A waltz," he said. "It appears I am saved." He bowed grandly to her and Olivia made a deep curtsy. He then took her into his arms and they began to dance. .

"You have remembered your instructions, my lord . . . that is to say, Gervas. You are doing very well."

"A man could not help but do well with you in his arms, Olivia," said the baron, gazing down into her enormous blue eyes.

An electric spark passed between them and neither one spoke. The baron was filled with a maddening longing for her. He wished only to clasp her to him and kiss her wildly. Olivia shared his excitement and realized that never before had she wanted a man as she did him.

So intent were they upon each other that they barely noted that the music had stopped. Ramsay continued to hold her in his arms, and then, noting that the others were watching them, he released her. "Thank you," he said softly. "And thank you for my dancing lesson, Olivia. I would not have wanted to miss that waltz."

She smiled up at him. "Nor would I, Gervas."

They met each other's gaze once more and then Ramsay offered her his arm. Joining Sophie and Aubrey, the baron and Olivia found them still standing with Malvern and the Horsleys.

"It is time to go in to supper," said Sophie, regarding her friend and Ramsay with keen interest. "I do hope this will go well."

"Of course it will, Sophie," said Olivia. "Don't be silly."

"Then let us start in," said Sophie.

"Would you do me the honor of going in with me, Lady Olivia?" said the baron, offering her his arm once again.

"Just a minute, Ramsay," said the squire. "You have had the last dance with Lady Olivia. I shall escort her to supper." He started to take Olivia's arm.

"I am taking Lady Olivia in," said Ramsay, eyeing Malvern with a menacing expression. "You had best find another partner."

The squire was taken aback by the baron's threatening manner. He bristled and clenched his fist belligerently. Sophie, alarmed that the two gentlemen appeared ready to come to blows, quickly intervened. "But, Mr. Malvern, I had thought that you might take me in. You are the master of the hunt and I am the hostess. You cannot disappoint me."

Malvern scowled at Ramsay, but then nodded to Sophie. "As you wish, Lady Roxbury," he said, extending his arm to her. A very relieved Sophie took it and started into the dining room with the big man. Olivia directed a grateful look at her friend and happily accompanied the baron in to supper.

19

The baron awoke to find the sun streaming into his bedchamber through the narrow opening in the curtains. Glancing at the mantel clock, he was surprised to find that it was nearly noon. It was most unusual for his lordship to have slept so late, but then it was not often that he danced until the early morning hours.

Ramsay smiled as he thought of the ball, realizing that he had never enjoyed himself so much. Being in Olivia's company and taking her in his arms had been wonderful. Smiling again, he thought of what it would be like to wake up and find her there beside him, her golden hair delightfully disheveled. Ramsay's fantasy was interrupted by a knock on the door. It opened and Burry peeked his head in. "Are you awake, my lad?"

Ramsay sat up in bed. "Come in, Professor. I was just getting up." Throwing off the bedcovers, the baron rose from the bed and put on his dressing gown.

Burry came in and, sitting down in a chair, grinned at his young friend. "So you are keeping town hours? I suspect that you are now lost to the academic world, since you will undoubtedly continue your nightly revels."

The baron laughed. "I confess that I might consider doing so if I knew that other nights would be as enjoyable."

The professor looked well satisfied with himself. "I knew I was right in urging you to go. Now, my boy, I am dying with anticipation. Tell me all about it."

"You sound like Geordie, sir."

Burry grinned. "Perhaps I should fetch him, too. I know he is most eager to learn of your adventures. The poor lad is hard at work on his sums."

"I shall tell him later." Ramsay went to the window and pulled open the curtains, allowing the bright light to flood the room. "What a glorious day."

"You are in a deuced good mood, Ramsay. I daresay it has something to do with Lady Olivia Dunbar."

"It has everything to do with her," said the baron, pacing across the room in some agitation. "By God, sir, I am in love with her."

"I am hardly shocked by the admission, my lad. And you have finally realized that she shares your feelings?"

Ramsay stopped his pacing. "I have reason to hope so, sir."

"Good, my boy, then you must go and see the lady. Ask her to marry you."

"You don't think she would consider me too abrupt?"

"Heavens no," replied Burry. "There is no point in beating about the bush. Go and see her."

"I will," said the baron resolutely, and then shouted for his servant.

The baron sat astride the enormous charger Destre and cantered toward Fenwyck. Ramsay was in extraordinary good spirits, for as he rode along he pictured his joyful existence with Olivia as his wife. He could scarcely wait to see her and was very glad to finally arrive at the Roxburys' residence.

His euphoric mood was quickly dashed when upon being shown into the drawing room, he found that he was not the only caller. Sitting beside Olivia on the sofa was Squire Malvern. Sir Aubrey and Lady Roxbury were there too, and the gentlemen rose as he came in. "Lord Ramsay," said Sophie, "how good of you to call. Do sit down."

After frowning at Malvern and smiling at Olivia, the baron took a chair. He realized that things were not working out as planned. Ramsay certainly had not expected the squire to be in attendance and he wondered how he would be able to speak to Olivia alone. "It was a wonderful ball, Lady Roxbury," said his lordship politely.

"Yes," said Sophie, "it did go very well."

"It certainly got the hunting season off to a good start," said Malvern. "We're hunting again tomorrow." Ramsay frowned but said nothing.

"We'll hope to catch one of the crafty beggars tomorrow," added Aubrey enthusiastically.

"A pity you'll not be riding, Ramsay," said the squire. "I should very much like to see this alleged horsemanship of yours."

Olivia looked indignant. "There is nothing alleged about it, Mr. Malvern."

"You must allow me a certain skepticism," returned the squire, smiling unpleasantly. "Ramsay and I have been acquainted for many years."

"A true and unfortunate fact of my life," said the baron.

Sophie quickly changed the subject. "And how is your nephew, Lord Ramsay? Such a charming young man. I imagine you'll be sending him to school soon?"

"He'll not send the cub to school," said Malvern scornfully. "He's too afraid it would make a man of him."

"You blackguard," said Ramsay, rising from his chair and glaring at the squire. "I'll not bear your insults, nor will I upset the Roxburys or Lady Olivia by quarreling with you. I shall return again when the noble master of the hunt is not here."

Nodding at the Roxburys and looking apologetically at

Olivia, the baron left abruptly. "Well, it appears I have flushed our monk from the covert," said Malvern with a triumphant grin.

Aubrey started to laugh at this remark but quickly stopped at the enraged expression on Olivia's face. "I think you are insufferable, Mr. Malvern," she said. "How can you speak to Lord Ramsay in such a manner?"

"I shall speak to him in any manner I please," replied the squire testily.

"I say, Malvern," said Aubrey, irritated at his guest's tone. "Perhaps you had better leave."

The squire looked as if he was about to make an angry retort, but he checked himself. "I didn't mean to upset you, Roxbury. It is just that the fellow makes me lose my temper. He always has."

Aubrey was appeased by Malvern's conciliatory tone, but both of the ladies regarded the squire with disapproval. "Then let us speak no more of Lord Ramsay," said the baronet. "I am looking forward to tomorrow's hunt."

"Aye," replied the squire. "I know we shall have a kill." He smiled at Olivia. "And I hope I shall be able to give the mask and brush to you."

"I fear that is quite impossible," said Olivia coolly, "for I shall not be riding with you tomorrow."

"What?" said Aubrey. "You are not hunting tomorrow, Livy?"

Olivia shook her head. "I shall remain here." She rose from her chair and directed an icy look at the squire. "Do excuse me. I must go and finish my book, *The Age of Chivalry*, by Lord Ramsay. It is a topic you obviously would little understand, Mr. Malvern." With these cutting words, she left them.

Malvern's face grew red and he glowered angrily. "It appears Ramsay has charmed your cousin, Roxbury. He must be a sorcerer as well as a monk."

Sophie smiled. "His lordship may be a monk now, Mr.

Malvern, but I daresay it is not his intention to remain one much longer.''

Aubrey chuckled at his wife's remark, but Malvern remained very grim. ''I hardly think it very amusing, Lady Roxbury. A girl like Lady Olivia deserves better than Ramsay.''

''How good of you to be so concerned with Olivia's welfare, Mr. Malvern,'' said Sophie, casting an ironic look at him.

The squire frowned but made no remark. Aubrey tried to turn the subject back to hunting, but Malvern was in a very ill temper and disinclined to talk even about his beloved hounds. After a short time, he left them.

When the squire had gone, Sophie shook her head. ''He is truly a dreadful man, Aubrey. I do wish he wasn't your friend.''

''But he is such a fine master of the hunt,'' replied the baronet defensively.

''I do not dispute that, but I'm sure that is his only virtue. What bad luck that Malvern was here when Ramsay appeared. I would not be surprised if the baron intended to ask Livy to marry him.''

''So you think the wager is won?'' asked Aubrey.

''Yes, is it not too funny? I can scarcely wait to write to my brother and tell him about it!'' She looked at her husband and noted that he did not appear too happy. ''What is the matter, my dear?''

Aubrey frowned. ''It is very well to win the wager, Sophie, but when the bet was first made, I had no idea that Livy would accept him. Good heavens, she will marry the fellow!''

Sophie laughed. ''And what is wrong with that? I admit that I was not overly fond of Ramsay when first we became acquainted with him, but now I believe I like him. And I know that Livy is in love with him and he with her. I fancy they will be very happy together.''

''Well, perhaps you are right, my dear.''

"Of course I'm right," said Sophie, smiling at the baronet. "I am a good judge of such things. After all, I knew that we would suit very well despite what your mother thought."

Aubrey grinned. "Yes, that is very true, my love. Well, Ramsay cannot be as bad as I originally thought. After all, he can certainly sit a horse."

Sophie laughed again and kissed her husband fondly.

20

The following afternoon Sophie entered Olivia's sitting room and found her friend sitting in a chair, Mayflower curled in her lap. The dog directed a questioning look as she came toward them waving a piece of paper. "Livy, there is a letter for you. It is from your sister-in-law."

"How wonderful," said Olivia ironically.

Sophie laughed and gave her friend the letter. When Olivia barely glanced at it, Lady Roxbury looked a trifle impatient. "Aren't you going to read it?"

Olivia shrugged and stroked the whippet. "Why should I ruin my day?"

"You are horrible," said Sophie, "and far too hard on your dear sister-in-law. I wish you would read it. I am starved for news."

"Oh, very well, but you know that Jocasta never includes any interesting gossip. And I daresay the duke's household is very dull indeed." Olivia broke the seal and perused the letter. "My nephew Ralph has got a new pony and has named it Jasper."

"That is news, Livy."

"The duke's gout is acting up and he is confined to bed."

"Poor man," said Sophie.

"Jocasta's sister is getting married to Lord Thomas Beach."

"And you said this letter would be dull," said Sophie, smiling. "It is surely newsworthy that the duke would allow his daughter to marry Lord Thomas Beach. In addition to that gentleman's great failing in being a second son, he is a notorious rake."

"The duke has always liked him," said Olivia, continuing to read the letter, "but Jocasta is not at all happy with the match. Here is what she says on the matter: 'Although I do not approve of Lord Thomas, I must admit that it is about time she married, and after all, a girl must not be too particular or she will find herself an old maid.' " Olivia smiled over at Sophie. "That is for my benefit." She continued reading from the letter. " 'It is such a pity that you did not come with us. Many of my sister's rejected suitors are about. I am certain, Olivia, that you are not finding any suitable gentleman in the north.' "

Sophie laughed. "I am so glad that you will be able to write back to Jocasta and tell her that you are engaged to Lord Ramsay."

"But I am not engaged."

"Not yet, but I suspect he intended to ask for your hand yesterday afternoon. He had that look about him. If Malvern had not been there, he would have done so. Oh, Livy, I am so happy for you."

Olivia smiled. "Then you do not disapprove?"

"How could I, when you are so fond of him? I find Ramsay a much more agreeable gentleman now than when we first met him in town."

Olivia laughed. "So do I," she said. "Oh, Sophie, I am so in love with him. You know, it is odd, but in the past, I was not at all eager to get married. Now I can barely wait until Gervas asks me."

"Then why do we stay here? Why don't we go to

Hawkesmuir and give your Gervas the opportunity to propose?''

"Oh, I don't know . . ." Olivia hesitated.

"Why, it is perfect. Aubrey will be gone for the rest of the afternoon. We cannot just sit around here being bored. Let us go to Hawkesmuir.''

Olivia paused, wondering if she should agree to do so. Then, thinking how much she wanted to see Ramsay, she nodded. "Very well.''

"Good," said Sophie. "Oh, this is so exciting. Now, don't dawdle, my dear. Your baron awaits!'' Olivia smiled and then she and Lady Roxbury hurried out of the room to go and change.

Professor Burry entered the library and found the baron sitting at his desk. Ramsay did not notice him, but stared absently into space. Unlike his master, Wolstan was immediately aware of Burry's presence and ambled over to him. The professor stroked the big dog's head fondly and smiled over at the baron. "Perhaps I should not disturb you, Ramsay.''

His lordship looked over at Burry in some surprise. "Professor, I did not see you come in.''

"No, you were obviously far too intent on your work.''

A slight smile appeared on Ramsay's face. "I must confess that I have not been able to keep my mind on my work.''

Burry grinned. "I know very well what is occupying your thoughts, my boy. Why don't you go to Fenwyck and see Lady Olivia?''

The baron shook his head. "The Malvern is hunting today. I'm sure Lady Olivia is out with them.''

"Then you must go to Fenwyck this evening.''

"That was my intention, sir, but it seems a deuced long time until then.''

The professor laughed. "I'll wager you'll survive, lad. But you must come with us. Geordie and I are going to

Tynborough Abbey. At this moment your nephew labors feverishly to finish his Latin translation. As soon as he is done, we are going on an outing. Do say you will come.''

"Very well, I think that would be a good idea.''

"Capital. Then I shall wait here with you until Geordie has completed his Tacitus.''

The professor had barely sat down in an armchair near the baron's desk when Geordie hurried into the room, a paper in his hand. "I have finished, Professor.''

"Finished already?'' Burry eyed the boy skeptically. "I daresay you have scarcely had time for that. I should like to see your paper, young sir.''

Geordie handed it to the professor and smiled at his uncle. "We are going to the abbey, Uncle Gervas. Could you not come with us? What a lark it will be.''

"Not so fast, young man,'' said the baron, trying to look appropriately stern. "You must not rush through your lessons. One does not hurriedly dash off a translation of Tacitus. No, indeed, one must try to do a good job before going off on larks in the countryside.''

Geordie looked a trifle crestfallen. "Yes, sir,'' he said meekly.

"Take a look at this, Ramsay,'' said Burry solemnly, handing his lordship Geordie's paper.

The baron frowned as he took the paper and began to read it. "The penmanship is sloppy,'' he commented, and Geordie looked uneasy as his uncle continued to study the work. The boy then glanced questioningly at the professor. Burry winked at him, and Geordie smiled, very much relieved. Ramsay looked up from the paper. "By my honor, this is excellent. You have done very well, Geordie.''

"You could not have done better yourself, Ramsay. Why, if the prospect of an excursion inspires the lad to do such work, I daresay I shall have to plan more of them.''

"I would like that, sir,'' said Geordie eagerly.

Burry laughed. "Well, then, let us not stand about.

Geordie, go tell Jem to bring round the carriage. Your uncle is coming with us."

"How famous!" cried Geordie, rushing off. The mastiff Wolstan barked and hurried after the boy.

Ramsay smiled and returned Geordie's work to Burry. "The penmanship is quite sloppy."

The professor grinned. "You are a hard taskmaster, Ramsay. Of course, I recall another pupil of mine whose papers were not always written in the neatest of hands."

The baron laughed. "Very well, I see I have no right to criticize Geordie's penmanship. I am glad to see him making such good progress."

"He is a clever lad. I would not be surprised if there are two scholars in the family."

The baron smiled ruefully. "My father never wanted even one. He did not think scholarship the province of gentlemen. I embarrassed him."

"Surely not, Ramsay," said the professor.

"It is true. He could never understand why I preferred my books to more gentlemanly pursuits such as hunting."

"But he was fond of you, lad."

The baron nodded. "He was, yet I always knew how much I disappointed him by not being like him. I do not want Geordie to feel obliged to follow in my footsteps if it is not his inclination to do so."

Burry smiled. "That is very wise of you, my boy. I know that your children will be fortunate to have such an understanding papa."

"Is it not premature to speak of my children, sir?" said Ramsay with a smile.

"Only a trifle."

"Well, I think I should be concerned with getting married first."

Burry laughed. "That is advisable."

At that moment the butler appeared in the library. "My lord, there are two ladies to see you, Lady Roxbury and Lady Olivia."

"Here? Now?" said the baron.

"Aye, my lord," returned the butler.

"Well, show them to the drawing room. No, show them in here, Hardy."

The elderly servant nodded, and as he left the library, a smile appeared on his face. It seemed the arrival of Lady Olivia Dunbar had had the expected impact on his master. Although Mr. Hardy strongly discouraged gossip below-stairs, the servants at Hawkesmuir were spending much time speculating about the baron and Lady Olivia.

After the butler had gone, Burry grinned at Ramsay. "So she prefers visiting you to hunting. I think that a very good sign." Ramsay did not reply, but hurriedly straightened his cravat. Burry laughed. "Don't worry, my lad, you look like a deuced Corinthian."

The baron cast a ludicrous glance at the professor and then the ladies entered the room. Although Sophie looked very well in her mauve walking dress and stylish bonnet, Ramsay barely noted her. He saw only Olivia. That lady looked extraordinarily lovely in her peach-colored silk dress with matching spencer. Atop her golden curls was a wide-brimmed leghorn hat trimmed with peach-colored satin.

Both gentlemen rose to their feet to greet the ladies. "This is an unexpected pleasure," said the baron.

"Oh, we felt like taking a ride, Lord Ramsay," said Sophie. "I hope you don't mind our calling on you."

"Indeed not," replied his lordship. "Lady Roxbury, I do not believe you have met Professor Burry. Professor, may I present Lady Roxbury?"

"Your servant, ma'am," said Burry, bowing gallantly over Sophie's hand.

"I am so very happy to meet you, Professor Burry. Olivia has told me so much about you. I am glad to meet such a learned man. Indeed, I do not think I have met any learned man, aside from his lordship, of course."

"And I do not often get to meet beautiful ladies, Lady Roxbury," returned Burry.

"Do sit down," said Ramsay, smiling at Olivia. After they were all seated in chairs near the fireplace, the baron turned to Olivia. "I thought you would be hunting. I know the Malvern is out."

She smiled at him. "I did not care to hunt today. I am not hunting mad, you know."

"Indeed not," said Sophie. "Olivia is not at all like my husband. I fear he lives for the sound of the huntsman's horn."

"Surely, Lady Roxbury," said Burry, "with a wife as lovely as yourself, hunting cannot be all he lives for."

Ramsay eyed the professor, rather surprised at his talent for flummery. Sophie appeared delighted. "Such flattery, sir, but I do own I like it. I shall have to meet more academic gentlemen."

Burry grinned, but before he could reply, Geordie and Wolstan rushed into the room. "The carriage is ready and—" Seeing the guests, he stopped abruptly. "Oh, I am sorry."

"Good morning, Geordie," said Olivia, smiling at the boy. The mastiff wagged his tail at seeing Olivia and went over to her. "And good morning to you, Wolstan."

"That is a very large dog," said Sophie, eyeing Wolstan dubiously.

"But he is so sweet," said Olivia, petting the dog. "He is quite harmless, Sophie."

"Oh, yes, Lady Roxbury," said Geordie, hastening to reassure her. "He would never hurt anyone he likes."

"Then I shall endeavor to be his friend," said Sophie, smiling at the boy. "But you said the carriage was ready. Are you going somewhere, young man?"

Geordie nodded. "Uncle Gervas, Professor Burry, and I are going to Tynborough Abbey."

"Then we have interrupted your plans," said Olivia. "We do not wish to detain you."

"Nonsense," said Ramsay.

"Why don't you come with us?" said Geordie. "It is a great lark."

Ramsay eyed his nephew disapprovingly. "Geordie, I don't think the ladies would be interested in going."

"But I would very much like to go," said Olivia. "I read about it in your book. Let me see, it was built in 1152 and destroyed by King Henry the Eighth in 1537. Poor Brother Sebastian died trying to defend it from the king's soldiers."

"He was beheaded," said Geordie, eager to add to the tale. "They say his ghost wanders about there, but I have never seen it."

"Oh dear," said Sophie, "that sounds quite dreadful. I am not at all fond of ghosts, especially headless ones."

"But that is only at night," said Geordie. "It is quite lovely in the daytime. We have picnics there."

Ramsay was surprised and impressed that Olivia had remembered about the abbey. He smiled at her. "If you ladies would like to come, you would be very welcome to do so."

Olivia looked over at Sophie, and although Lady Roxbury was not eager to visit a ruin possibly inhabited by a ghost, she readily agreed. Surely, reasoned Sophie, there would be much opportunity on such an excursion for Ramsay and Olivia to have some time alone. Indeed, decided Lady Roxbury, she would make certain that the baron had a chance to propose.

A short time later the five of them were in Ramsay's carriage on their way to the abbey. Burry entertained them with details about their destination and Sophie asked him numerous questions about it. Olivia and Ramsay smiled at each other, barely listening to the professor.

The abbey ruin was not far and it did not take long to reach it. Nestled in the wooded hills, the old monastery was a picturesque sight. Much of it was still standing and it was easy to imagine what it must have looked like before its destruction. "It's beautiful," said Olivia.

"Yes, it is very nice," said Sophie, happy to find it such a pleasant place.

"Yes, it is," said Burry, and as they descended from the carriage, the professor began to discourse on the role of the monastery in feudal society. The professor offered Sophie his arm as they started off to tour the ruins. Taking his friend's example, Ramsay extended his arm to Olivia, who took it gladly. They roamed about for some time and Burry lectured about medieval life. Every so often the professor would direct a question to the baron, and Ramsay, who was totally engrossed with Olivia, would manage some sort of reply. However, the professor was not at all irked by the baron's inattention. On the contrary, he was very pleased to observe his young friend and Lady Olivia, and he had little doubt that Ramsay would soon be a married man.

They wandered about the monastery graveyard and Burry pointed out the spot where, according to tradition, the courageous Brother Sebastian was buried. After telling the monk's story, the professor nodded. "I believe we have seen everything. Everything but the kitchen, of course. We passed it back there, but did not stop. It is very interesting. I shall show you that now."

"My dear professor," said Sophie, "I fear I am quite exhausted. I think it best if I rest here for a time. I shall sit on the stone wall."

"Of course, Lady Roxbury," said Burry solicitously. "I apologize for overtiring you. We shall rest at once."

"But Livy is not at all tired and I know how much she would like to see the abbey kitchen." Sophie smiled at Ramsay. "Perhaps you could show it to her, my lord? Professor Burry will stay with me here."

"I shall come too," said Geordie. "I like seeing the kitchen."

"Oh, I thought you would keep me company too, Geordie," said Sophie. "I would like to talk to you."

"Yes, you stay with us, young sir," said the professor,

knowing very well that Lady Roxbury wanted Lady Olivia and the baron to be alone.

Geordie nodded and followed Burry and Sophie to the stone wall. Olivia could hardly hide her amusement at this obvious ploy. "Shall we go to see the kitchen, Lord Ramsay?" The baron smiled and they walked off. "I fear, Gervas, that Sophie is rather transparent. She wanted us to be alone."

"I am heartily grateful to her. There is so much I have to say to you, Olivia. I could not believe my good fortune when you and Lady Roxbury came this morning. I truly thought you would be hunting."

"I would much rather be with you."

The baron would have taken Olivia into his arms at that moment, but for the knowledge that they were within sight of the others. They continued on, soon arriving at the kitchen, a stone building in a remarkably good state of preservation. Olivia peered inside. "It is rather dark in there."

Ramsay smiled again. "Are you afraid that poor Brother Sebastian might be inside? It is a possibility, for they say he was exceedingly stout."

Olivia laughed. "I am willing to venture inside as long as you are with me. I do have such an interest in medieval kitchens."

"Then you must see the kitchens at Hawkesmuir Castle," said the baron, taking her arm and escorting her inside.

Once within the old building's stone walls, Olivia glanced about, noting the faint light coming in through a small window. "I daresay I am glad I wasn't a cook here." She looked over at Ramsay and saw that he was now regarding her with a serious expression.

"Olivia, I am sure that you cannot be unaware of the feelings I have for you. I can only hope that you would return a small portion of them."

She took his hands. "Oh, Gervas," she murmured, looking up at him.

The baron needed no further prompting. He gathered her into his arms and covered her lips with his own. They kissed long and passionately, and then, pausing only to catch their breath, their lips sought each other's again.

"Who's in there?" cried a masculine voice and, startled, Olivia and Ramsay pulled apart. "I say, who's in there?"

"What the deuce," muttered Ramsay darkly, looking toward the source of the interruption. There at the small window was a man's face peering in at them. "Who the devil are you?"

"I am Mr. Simms. Who are you?"

"I am Ramsay."

"Lord Ramsay! 'Pon my faith, what good luck this is! I was just coming to see you, my lord."

Olivia righted her bonnet, which had fallen backward during their passionate embrace. Now recovered from the shock of Mr. Simms's untimely appearance, she found the situation rather amusing. Simms ran from the window to the door and hurried inside. "Yes, Lord Ramsay, I was on my way to call upon you and . . ." The young curate stopped as he caught sight of Olivia in the dim light. "Oh, Lady Olivia."

Olivia nearly laughed at the shocked expression on Simms's lean face. "Lord Ramsay was showing me the abbey kitchen. It is most interesting."

"Yes, it is," said the curate awkwardly.

"Did you not see Professor Burry, Lady Roxbury, and young Master Sinclair out there?" said Olivia.

"No," said Simms. "I came from the woods." He looked over at Ramsay and noted the unhappy expression on the baron's face. "I am sorry to interrupt you, my lord. Do excuse me."

Feeling rather sorry for the curate, Olivia smiled at him.

"Oh, you were not really interrupting. We were just about to join the others. Were we not, Lord Ramsay?"

"Yes, of course," said the baron ill-temperedly.

"Perhaps Mr. Simms could accompany us back to Hawkesmuir Castle, could he not, my lord?" She smiled over at him and Ramsay tried to forget his annoyance with Mr. Simms. After all, it was very clear that Olivia Dunbar reciprocated his feelings. He smiled at the curate.

"Yes, Mr. Simms, do come back with us. You have not yet met Professor Burry, and I know he will be glad to meet you."

"Thank you, my lord," said the curate, seemingly relieved. Simms turned to leave, and after exchanging a glance, Olivia and the baron followed.

21

Sophie glanced out the carriage window as the vehicle made its way toward Fenwyck. She then looked at her friend. "I think it very bad of Mr. Simms to have come upon you when he did, Livy."

Olivia smiled. "I did think his appearance very ill-timed. The poor man. He was so embarrassed."

"He seemed to recover well enough. He was quite eager to accompany us back to Hawkesmuir and bore us all with his talk."

"Oh, Sophie, I did not think Mr. Simms at all boring."

"Well, I do not fancy that the murder of Thomas à Becket in the year 1170 is a fit topic for tea."

"Perhaps not, but it was not dull."

"You are far more charitable toward that young man than I. Your baron did not appear at all pleased with him. Indeed, the way he was looking at Simms, I thought the curate might meet the same fate as Thomas à Becket." Olivia laughed and Sophie continued. "Well, it is a pity that Simms appeared, for I suspect that if he had not, you would now be engaged to Lord Ramsay and a very happy woman."

"Oh, Sophie, I am a happy woman."

Sophie took her friend's hand and squeezed it. "I am so pleased for you, Livy. And since Ramsay promised to call at Fenwyck tomorrow, I know we can expect him early. Perhaps it is just as well that you will have some time to think about your response to the baron's offer."

Olivia smiled again. "I assure you, I need no time for that, Sophie."

"I didn't think you would," replied her friend, and as the carriage continued on, Sophie began to talk excitedly about Olivia's wedding plans.

With such a pleasant and interesting subject of conversation, the trip back to the Roxbury residence seemed very short. After returning to the country home, Sophie retired to her rooms for a nap. Olivia sat in the drawing room working absently on her embroidery. She added but a few stitches to her floral pattern, for she was so engrossed in her thoughts of Ramsay. Olivia smiled as she thought of their embrace in the abbey kitchen and blushed as she remembered the baron's hot kisses.

The sound of men's voices interrupted her reflections. "Good God, Roxbury, I've never seen a finer kill!"

"Nor have I, Malvern. What a grand moment it was!" Squire Malvern and Sir Aubrey entered the drawing room. Attired in their scarlet hunting coats, they appeared in the highest of spirits. The baronet grinned at his cousin. "You missed a fine hunt, Livy. Oh, it was glorious."

"Aye, it was," said Malvern enthusiastically. "What a shame you were not riding, Lady Olivia."

"Indeed it was," said Aubrey. "Lady Horsley was asking for you. By God, that woman can sit a horse. She received the brush from today's kill."

"And well she deserved it," said the squire, very proud of his sister.

"But we must not make my cousin feel too bad about not riding, Malvern. We have had a splendid time, while she has doubtless spent a very tedious day. But where is Sophie?"

"She went to take a nap, Aubrey."

"Then it must have been very dull," remarked the baronet.

"Indeed not," said Olivia. "Sophie was quite tired after our expedition."

"Expedition?" Aubrey regarded his cousin in surprise.

Olivia nodded. "Sophie and I accompanied Lord Ramsay, Professor Burry, and Geordie to Tynborough Abbey."

"That ruin?" said Malvern. "It is the dullest place in the county. You have my sympathy, Lady Olivia, for having to endure such a trip in such company."

Olivia frowned at the big man. "Both Lady Roxbury and I enjoyed ourselves very much."

Aubrey regarded her skeptically. "I never thought you were the sort to poke about ruins, and I know dashed well that Sophie ain't the type to do so."

"Your wife probably just enjoyed being in the company of such charming gentlemen, Roxbury," said the squire sarcastically.

Sir Aubrey laughed and Olivia directed a warning look at him, but before she could reply, a servant entered the drawing room. "Your pardon, Sir Aubrey, but Mr. Taylor is here to see you about a horse."

"Oh, I have been wanting to see him," said the baronet.

"Take care, Roxbury," said Malvern, "Taylor is a shrewd horse trader. He'll try to sell you the damnedest hack."

"I shall heed your warning, Malvern," replied Aubrey. He looked at his cousin. "Would you mind entertaining Mr. Malvern, Livy? I shall only be a short time with Taylor."

Although not at all eager to comply with this request, Olivia nodded. Aubrey left them and the squire deposited his large frame on the sofa near her chair. "I must say that I think it fortunate that Taylor has chosen this time to appear. I don't have much opportunity to be alone with you." Olivia made no reply to this remark and Malvern continued. "So you were with Ramsay today, were you? And to think you could have been hunting."

"I assure you I much preferred calling at Hawkesmuir and going to the abbey."

He shook his head and regarded her incredulously. "Oh, yes, I know how much you enjoy Ramsay's company. For the life of me, I cannot see what appeal such a man has for a woman like you. Indeed, it seems to me that Ramsay's only virtue is the fatness of his purse."

Olivia eyed him indignantly. "It is obvious that you do not know Lord Ramsay very well."

"I know him much better than I care to. But let's not talk about him. I don't want to quarrel with you."

The squire's abrupt change of tone made Olivia somewhat wary. "I'm glad of that, Mr. Malvern," she said.

"Ah, now we are getting along much better." He smiled. "We are really very well suited, you and I."

Olivia arched her eyebrows. "Indeed?"

"Of course we are. We both love horses and hounds and a good chase across rough country." Malvern grinned at Olivia. "And I'll be bound, you'll find hunting is not the only sport at which I excel and which you'd find to your liking."

Olivia reddened and wished that Aubrey had not left. "I fear I must disappoint you, sir, for I find little similarity between us."

"That is only because you deny it, my girl," said the squire. "A young female like you may think she prefers a bloodless fellow like Ramsay, but once married to such a one, you'll soon wish you had a man in your bed."

Rising angrily to her feet, Olivia glared at him. "How dare you! I shall not listen to you a moment longer."

Olivia started to go, but jumping up, Malvern grabbed her arm. "Not so fast, my lady. I see you have need of a bit more persuasion." Malvern's grip tightened on her arm and he only laughed at the alarmed look on her face. Then suddenly the squire pulled her to him and kissed her brutally. When he finally released Olivia, she gasped for breath. "You see?" he said triumphantly. "That's the way a man does it."

Olivia regarded his grinning face with astonishment and then with all the force she could muster, she slapped him hard across the face. "A man! You are not a man, but a brutish oaf!"

Malvern was stunned by the force of her blow. He growled and grabbed her wrist again. "No one treats Roger Malvern like that."

Olivia wrenched her arm from his grasp and hurried away from him. As she rushed from the drawing room into the corridor, she nearly collided with her cousin.

"Good Lord, Livy, what is the matter?" cried the baronet, alarmed at her expression.

"Ask your friend, Aubrey!" said Olivia, her voice trembling with fury. "I never want to see that man again!" Without another word, she ran past him and soon vanished from sight.

The very puzzled baronet entered the drawing room and found the squire standing by the fireplace rubbing his jaw. "What in God's name happened, Malvern? Livy was in a devil of a state. You had best explain yourself."

"Don't fly up into the boughs, Roxbury. It was nothing."

"My cousin did not seem to think so. You obviously upset her."

The squire shrugged. "Perhaps I did lose my head, but upon my honor, there was no cause for her to be in the high fidgets. All I did was kiss her."

"See here, Malvern, if you think you can take liberties with my cousin . . ."

"A kiss is all it was. By God, can't you understand the effect your cousin has on a man? I think I might be excused one small lapse in decorum. She slapped me soundly for my efforts. And don't go on with some drivel about meeting me on the field of honor. I have no wish to kill you, Roxbury, and lose the newest member of the Malvern Hunt.''

Aubrey smiled. "I daresay Livy made too much of it, but I cannot have you treating her so in my house.''

"I do apologize, Roxbury, and shall control myself in the future. But you know how I feel about your cousin.''

Aubrey nodded. "Well, Livy has had such an effect on many gentlemen. I suppose you can be forgiven such a minor infraction. Let us speak no more of it. Come, Taylor has brought a horse. I need your opinion.''

Glad that the baronet had quickly forgiven him, Malvern grinned and the two men left the drawing room. After some time they returned, and from Aubrey's expression it was clear he was very pleased with himself. "I'm in your debt, Malvern. To get such a horse at such a price is a marvel. We must celebrate!'' The baronet rang for his servant and instructed him to bring a bottle of his best port from the cellar.

Sometime later both gentlemen were ensconced on the sofa, downing the wine appreciatively. Soon Aubrey was in an even better mood, chattering happily to the squire. "Well, I think it is a damn pity that my cousin prefers Ramsay to you, old man.''

Malvern frowned at this remark and watched the baronet finish his glass of wine. Sir Aubrey was never a man to hold his liquor and he was rapidly becoming inebriated. "Are you so sure she prefers him to me?''

Aubrey nodded and poured another glass of wine. "Deuced odd, ain't it? Whoever would have thought that my cousin would lose her heart to such a man? Why, in town she could have her choice of any gentleman.'' He suddenly burst into laughter. "Damn me, if it ain't the result of that wager.''

"Wager?'' Malvern eyed the baronet curiously.

A silly grin appeared on Aubrey's rabbity countenance. "Yes, a wager. You see, when we were at a party in town, Livy made a joke about marrying the next man who came into the room." Aubrey laughed. "How funny it was when the next man happened to be dear old Monk Ramsay. I had met him, of course, and told Livy she could not have found a worse candidate for husband. Sophie's brother doubted that even Livy could charm the fellow, and I wagered him one hundred pounds that she would have Ramsay offering for her by Christmas."

Malvern eyed the baronet in astonishment. "You mean it is some sort of game?"

"It was at first. Why, we pursued Ramsay about town, even following him to the British Museum. They've mummies there, you know. Then we asked him to dinner so Livy would have more opportunity to ensnare him. It was so awfully funny because Livy took an instant dislike to him and he seemed totally immune to her charms. How she came to like the man, I don't know. But I've never seen her so fond of any gentleman and I do expect she'll marry him." Aubrey laughed again. "And it is all the result of that silly wager."

"Does Ramsay know about this wager?" asked the squire.

"Good heavens, no." Aubrey suddenly seemed to realize he had been indiscreet. "What I tell you, Malvern, is, of course, in the strictest confidence."

"Of course, Roxbury," said the squire. He rose to his feet. "Well, Roxbury, I must be going."

Aubrey regarded him in surprise. "Oh, you must stay and finish the bottle."

"No, I have to be going, Roxbury. We hunt again tomorrow, and I shall see you then." Malvern took his leave, and as he departed Fenwyck, a malicious smile appeared on his face.

22

Baron Ramsay sat in a comfortable armchair before the fire awaiting dinner. Wolstan sat on the floor beside him, looking very happy as his master stroked his enormous head. Ramsay smiled slightly as he stared into the flames. Despite Mr. Simms's unwanted appearance that day and the baron's failure to ask Olivia to be his bride, his lordship was not at all disheartened. Indeed, he could scarcely be in a better mood. The lovely Olivia had made it clear that she returned his feelings and it would just be a matter of time before she would be mistress of Hawkesmuir Castle.

The baron looked down at his dog. "Well, Wolstan, your master will soon be a married man. I know you're already fond of Olivia." The mastiff regarded Ramsay questioningly, as if trying to understand the baron's words. Ramsay laughed and scratched Wolstan behind the ears. "Of course, we may have to live in London part of the year, but I daresay we shall both grow accustomed to it." Wolstan did not look at all unhappy at the prospect of living in the great metropolis. He grinned up at his master, who laughed again. "I am a very fortunate man, Wolstan."

Ramsay stared once again at the fire and grew reflective. He barely noted the entrance of his butler. "Excuse me, m'lord." The baron looked up. "You have a caller. Mr. Malvern."

"Malvern here?" The butler's expression showed that he, too, thought it most odd for the squire to appear at Hawkesmuir Castle. "What the devil could he want?" Ramsay frowned. "I suppose I shall have to find out. Send him in here, Hardy."

"Very good, m'lord," said the servant, bowing and leaving the room.

Ramsay could think of no reason for Malvern's call and he eyed the big man curiously as the squire entered the library. The baron rose stiffly to his feet. "Malvern."

"Ramsay," replied the squire, appearing quite jovial. "I'm sure you did not expect me to visit you."

"No, I did not, but I suppose there must be some purpose in your coming. I suggest you state it."

"You are blunt, Ramsay. I shall come to the point, then. I don't want to waste your time. I know how busy you are writing those tomes of yours. Aren't you going to ask me to sit down?"

"Do as you will," muttered the baron. The squire grinned and took a seat. Ramsay reluctantly sat down as well. The mastiff directed a wary gaze at the intruder, sensing that Malvern was not welcome. "Well?" said Ramsay a trifle impatiently.

"I have just come from Fenwyck, where I have heard a most interesting story. Since I knew you would be very eager to hear it, I made haste to call upon you."

"I cannot think of anything you might say to me that would be of the least interest."

The squire grinned unpleasant. "Even if it concerns Lady Olivia Dunbar?"

"Especially if it concerns her."

Malvern shook his head. "I cannot understand you, Ramsay. I come here out of Christian charity with information of great interest to you, and you do not wish to hear it. Very well, I shall just allow Lady Olivia to win her wager and make a fool of you."

"What are you talking about?"

"So I have piqued your interest. I am glad of it."

"Tell me what you have come here to say and have done with it."

The squire nodded. "Sir Aubrey Roxbury told me of a wager placed in town. You know, of course, that the Roxburys and Lady Olivia Dunbar move in the first circles of London society and such things are common there. It seems that on a certain day they were attending a party, and to amuse themselves they made a wager that Lady Olivia could make a certain difficult gentleman fall in love with her and make her an offer by Christmas. I don't have to tell you who that gentleman was."

"What rubbish, Malvern. I suggest you leave."

"I know how it would upset any man's vanity to hear this, but it is the truth. Did you not think it odd how they followed you about town? Did you not wonder at their interest? Roxbury said they even came to the British Museum in search of you. I do not doubt that Lady Olivia thought it very funny trying to ensnare you. I'm sure you were her greatest challenge, but it seems she has succeeded admirably. I daresay you were gulled into thinking she cares for you. I feel sorry for you, Ramsay, for I do not like seeing a woman make a fool of any man, especially such a pathetic fellow as you."

Ramsay rose from his chair. Livid with rage, he strove to control his anger. "Get out of here, Malvern," he managed to say. "You are never to set foot inside my door again."

The squire laughed. "That is punishment indeed, my lord."

"Get out, damn you!" shouted the baron, no longer able to hide his fury.

Wolstan, seeing that there was an enemy in their midst, positioned himself in front of the baron and growled menacingly at the squire. The sight of the enormous mastiff poised to attack completely unnerved Malvern. "For God's sake, Ramsay, call off your dog."

"Get out or by God you will know what it feels like to be a fox in your damned hunt!"

Keeping his eyes on Wolstan, Malvern rose slowly from his chair and backed out of the room. Upon reaching the door of the library, he turned and scurried off. The mastiff barked loudly and started after the squire, but the baron's stern command brought him quickly back.

Ramsay frowned and walked over to stand in front of the fire. Did Malvern think he would believe his despicable lies? he asked himself. "Damn him to hell," said Ramsay aloud. He paced across the room, suddenly filled with doubts. He thought back to London and his first meeting with Olivia and the Roxburys. He had considered it strange that they had singled him out for their attention. Indeed, he had suspected at that time that they were making sport of him.

Perhaps Malvern's story was not so preposterous. It definitely would explain the events in town. The baron's expression grew grim. Could Olivia be feigning her interest in him, playing a part like a London actress? Could she be laughing at him behind his back, thinking him the most gullible of fellows?

Ramsay tried to dismiss the idea as absurd, but his suspicions continued to nag at him. He must find out the truth, he resolved. He would go to Olivia at once and ask her about the wager.

"Pardon me, m'lord, but dinner is ready."

"What?" The baron turned to face his butler and regarded him with a strange expression.

"Is something wrong, m'lord?"

"No, Hardy, but I must go out."

"Now, m'lord?" The servant looked bewildered.

"Professor Burry and Master Geordie must not wait for me. Have them eat dinner."

Hardy nodded, and the baron hurried past him out of the library.

*   *   *

Dinner at Fenwyck was unusually subdued. At most times the evening meal was marked by laughter and conversation. However, that night the three friends were uncommonly quiet. Olivia was still consumed with thoughts of Ramsay and she scarcely noticed the elaborate repast before her.

Sophie was peeved with her husband for drinking to excess that afternoon. She expressed her displeasure with an icy silence. The baronet thought his wife's attitude unreasonable, insisting that he was not in the least bit foxed. He did not feel very well, and that combined with Sophie's coolness made dinner that evening quite unpleasant for Aubrey.

The baronet took a forkful of poached salmon, but eyeing it midway to his mouth, he blanched and set it down again. The butler chose that moment to approach him. "I beg your pardon, sir, but Lord Ramsay is here wishing to see Lady Olivia. He is waiting in the drawing room."

"Here at this hour? Has he no manners?" grumbled Aubrey. "Tell him we are at dinner."

"I did tell him that, sir, but he said that it was urgent that he see Lady Olivia at once. His lordship seemed most agitated, sir."

Olivia looked over at Sophie. "I must see him, of course."

"Good heavens, cousin," said Aubrey. "Let him wait."

"Aubrey, you are terrible," said Sophie. "It is obvious that poor Ramsay cannot bear to wait a moment longer to ask for Livy's hand. She must see him immediately."

"Do as you wish, Livy," muttered the baronet. "You would in any case, but I think it a ramshackle business."

Olivia smiled at Sophie and then hurried from the dining room. As she approached the drawing room, her heart raced at the prospect of seeing Ramsay again. She passed through the doorway and saw the baron standing there looking out a window. "Gervas," said Olivia, smiling. He turned around and she was startled by his distraught expression. "What is wrong?"

"Olivia, I must talk with you."

"Of course, please sit down."

"I prefer to stand, thank you."

Olivia regarded the baron in concern. "It is obvious that something is the matter. Do tell me what is wrong."

Ramsay paused before he spoke. "Malvern called upon me at Hawkesmuir a short time ago."

"Malvern?" Olivia looked surprised.

He nodded. "He told me something, which I hope with all my heart is not true. It is about you, Olivia."

"Me? What could he have said about me? I would very much like to hear whatever he has said to upset you."

"He told me that you and the Roxburys had made a wager that I could be persuaded to ask for your hand by Christmastime." The baron was watching Olivia's expression intently as he made this statement. Her reaction confirmed his worst suspicions. "Then it is true?"

"Oh, Gervas, there was a wager, but I assure you—"

"That is all I need to know, madam. Further explanation is not necessary."

"But it is! Oh, Gervas, surely you cannot think so little of me that you could believe that my feelings for you are not genuine."

"What is the matter, my lady? I know how hard it must be for you to lose your wager when your goal was so close at hand. Good God, what a mindless dupe I have been!"

"You are wrong! I swear to you that you are wrong!" Olivia tried to take his arm, but he pulled away.

"I had thought it very odd in London that a woman like you would show such interest in me." He smiled a hard, cynical smile. "I had at first taken you for a fortune huntress, but after learning that you would have a large marriage settlement, I was quite perplexed. Now I understand. It was just a game to you, trying to entice the eccentric baron into making a fool of himself. Thank God that I did not ask you to marry me and have been spared the further humiliation of having you laugh in my face.''

"Oh, Gervas, how can you think that! I admit that at first it was a game, and I know it was very wrong of me. But I called off the wager long ago. I love you, Gervas!''

"You may spare yourself the theatrics, madam, although I own your performance has been quite commendable.''

"How can you not believe me?'' cried Olivia.

"How can I ever believe you?'' he returned. "I know now that I have misjudged you. You are just another deceitful, scheming female. I don't think you could ever care for anyone.''

Olivia's horror turned suddenly to anger. "How can you say such horrible things to me? If you love me, you could not believe this of me.''

The baron's look was glacial. "I don't recall, madam, ever saying that I loved you.''

Olivia reddened. "Then you don't love me?''

A mocking smile came to his face. "You are very sure of your charms, Lady Olivia.'' Olivia was momentarily too stunned to speak. "I think we have nothing further to say to each other,'' continued Ramsay. "Good evening, madam.''

"Go, then, my lord, if you are determined to be so pigheaded. Perhaps it is best that we part, since it is clear that you think so little of me.''

"I suggest you return to your conquest of sporting gentlemen. It will be much more amusing for you to spend your time with men who share your love of gaming.'' Casting one last glance at her, the baron stalked off.

Olivia watched him go, and then, throwing herself on the sofa, she broke into sobs.

23

"I daresay Livy has been gone a deuced long time," grumbled Sir Aubrey over his apple tart.

Sophie, who was still irked with her husband, frowned. "It has not been very long, Aubrey."

"Well, I don't like it. It hardly seems proper for her to be alone with Ramsay. I think we should join them."

"We will do nothing of the kind," replied Sophie sharply.

"I fancy her brother would be very vexed with me for not looking after her properly."

Lady Roxbury regarded her husband with annoyance. "What? Is Livy an infant that needs looking after? You are absurd, Aubrey."

The baronet made no reply, but stared sulkily down at his plate. Aubrey did not know when he had had a more unpleasant dinner. He and Sophie rarely quarreled, and until this time, Sir Aubrey had thought his was one of the most ideal of marriages. Now it appeared that Sophie was becoming one of those nagging wives who chide a man for his drinking and choice of friends.

The two sat in silence, and when the butler appeared in the dining room, Aubrey motioned to him. "Lord Ramsay is keeping Lady Olivia overlong. Tell them to join us."

"But, sir, his lordship left some time ago."

Aubrey eyed his servant in surprise. "Then why has Lady Olivia not returned to the dining room?"

"I fear, sir, her ladyship appeared upset. She said she wished to be alone."

"Oh dear," said Sophie, "whatever could have happened? We must go to her, Aubrey."

The baronet nodded and they hastily rose from the table and hurried to find Olivia. Entering the drawing room, Aubrey and Sophie were alarmed to see Olivia seated on the sofa, her face buried in her handkerchief. Sophie ran over to her. "Livy, what is wrong?"

Olivia raised her tearstained face to her friend. "Oh, Sophie," she said, but, breaking into sobs, she was unable to continue.

"There, there, my dear," said Sophie, placing a comforting arm around her friend's shoulders. "You must tell us what happened."

"What did Ramsay do, cousin?" asked Aubrey, a worried expression on his face. "By God, he will answer to me if he offended you!"

"Cease your nonsense, Aubrey," said Sophie impatiently, "and allow her to speak."

Finally regaining her self-control, Olivia dabbed at her eyes with her handkerchief. "Lord Ramsay will have nothing to do with me," she said.

"Whatever do you mean?" said Sophie. "Why, he is in love with you."

Olivia shook her head. "If ever he had any such feelings for me, I assure you they are gone. He hates me now."

"That is preposterous," said Aubrey. "The man is clearly besotted with you. Of course, I always thought him an odd fish. If he is so changeable, you are fortunate to be rid of him."

Olivia regarded the baronet angrily. "I should be thankful if you said nothing, Aubrey. I know it is you who must have told Malvern.''

Aubrey looked startled. "Told Malvern? What do you mean?''

"Do not look so innocent. Do you deny that you told Malvern about the wager?''

Sophie eyed her husband with astonishment. "Aubrey, you told Malvern about that?''

The baronet reddened. "I might have mentioned something about it to him.''

"I thought so,'' said Olivia, smiling ruefully. "The squire lost no time in carrying the tale to Gervas. Malvern told him that I only feigned interest in him, that I was merely pretending to care for him so that I might win the accursed wager! Oh, I have hurt him terribly.''

"Aubrey, I cannot believe you could have done such a despicable thing!'' cried Sophie.

The baronet looked defensive. "Perhaps I was indiscreet and perhaps I was a trifle foxed, but I told Malvern the information was in strict confidence. How was I to know that he would run to Ramsay?''

"You are a simpleton as well as a gabster,'' said Sophie angrily. "You know Malvern hates Ramsay. I'm sure he was only too eager to tell him something he knew would devastate him.''

"But I made it very clear to Malvern that although the business started as a wager, Livy had come to be very fond of Ramsay. Indeed, I told him that I thought it ironic that now she wished to marry the baron.''

Sophie frowned. "You can be certain that Malvern neglected to mention that part of the story.'' She turned to Olivia. "But surely you can explain this to Ramsay.''

"He will not believe me. I tried very hard to tell him the truth, but I had to admit that there had been a wager at first. Oh, if you had seen his face! He will never forgive me! And then we had angry words as well! I shall never see him again!'' Olivia burst into tears and Aubrey and Sophie exchanged glances.

"You must know how sorry I am,'' said the baronet. "I shall go at once to Hawkesmuir and explain the whole matter to Ramsay.''

"I think you have done quite enough, Aubrey,'' said Sophie. At his pained expression, she softened. "It would serve nothing for you to speak to him when he is in a temper. Perhaps when he is cooled and is more reasonable, you could see him.'' She sighed. "I daresay you are not the only one at fault. My brother and I thought the wager so very amusing. It was quite wicked to make sport of poor Ramsay in town. Now that I know him, I feel quite ashamed.''

"He is right to despise me,'' said Olivia miserably.

"Nonsense,'' said Sophie. "My dear Livy, you must not be so upset. I know you will make things right with Ramsay.''

Olivia shook her head. "No, there is no hope of that.'' She rose from her chair. "Do not worry about me. I must have some time alone now. I shall go to my sitting room.''

"Livy,'' said the baronet, a stricken look on his face, "I am so sorry.''

Olivia smiled at her cousin. "I know, Aubrey. I do not blame you so much as I blame myself. I pray you both excuse me.'' She left the drawing room and Aubrey slumped down on the sofa.

"I have made a muddle of things, Sophie.''

Sophie sat down beside him and placed a sympathetic hand on her husband's shoulder. "I know you never meant to hurt Livy. I am sorry for being so sharp with you, my dear.''

Seeing that Sophie had forgiven him, a look of tremendous relief came to the baronet's face. "Sophie, my darling, I have been such a fool. I daresay you and Livy were right about Malvern. The fellow is no gentleman, to be sure.''

Sophie smiled and kissed him. "At least some good has come out of this. You have learned the squire's true character. I do not think you will be so friendly to him in the future."

"I shall have nothing to do with him. If he dares show his face here, I shall not receive him."

"But, my dearest Aubrey, what of the Malvern Hunt?"

"The devil take it!" cried Aubrey. "I shall never ride with Malvern again, nor will I support it with my purse!"

Sophie regarded her husband in amazement. "You would give up hunting?"

"Good God, no," said Aubrey, looking at Sophie as if she were the greatest goosecap. "But the Malvern is not the only hunt. Why, I shall apply to the Duke of Northumberland to ride to his hounds."

Sophie eyed her husband with amusement and then laughingly embraced him.

"Professor Burry," said Geordie, who was sitting in the library near that gentleman, "it is quite late. Shouldn't my uncle be home?"

Burry looked up from his book. "There is no need to worry, my boy. His lordship will be here shortly."

"But where could he have gone? It is not at all like Uncle to miss dinner and go off without saying where he is going." Geordie directed a worried look at the professor. "It is not safe out at night. There are highwaymen about."

"Your uncle and Destre are more than a match for any highwayman, lad. Now, do not fear, he will come back soon." Although Professor Burry tried to speak confidently, he was himself concerned about the baron's inexplicable departure. He thought it most uncharacteristic of Ramsay to rush off without a word of explanation and did think it was growing rather late. While Geordie was occupied in petting Wolstan, Professor Burry glanced at the clock and frowned.

Then suddenly Wolstan lifted his enormous head and let

out a bark. "Is it Uncle?" said Geordie, looking toward the library door. The dog answered him by barking again and dashing to the door. "It is Uncle," said Geordie, leaping to his feet excitedly and hurrying to meet Ramsay as he entered the room. "You are safe!" cried Geordie, hugging the baron.

"Of course I'm safe," said his lordship, smiling down at the boy.

"I was worried. There are highwaymen about, you know."

"I am glad to say that I did not see any," said Ramsay.

"But where did you go, Uncle Gervas?"

"For a ride. I hope you and the professor were having a pleasant evening, but it is getting to be time for you to go to bed, young man."

"But, uncle, you have only just got home!"

"Go on, lad. To bed with you."

Geordie sensed from his uncle's tone that the baron would not relent. He nodded reluctantly and took his leave of the professor and Ramsay. When the boy had gone, the baron sat down wearily in a chair by the fire and absently laid a hand on his mastiff's head.

"Well, Ramsay, are you going to tell me about it!" said the professor.

The baron glanced over at him. "There is nothing to tell."

"I would have thought there was a great deal to tell, my boy. You acted deuced odd this evening."

"Very well, sir, I shall tell you. I have been out riding in the darkness after seeing Lady Olivia at Fenwyck."

"Good God," cried Burry, "you cannot mean that she has refused you!"

"I did not give her that opportunity, Professor."

"What on earth do you mean?"

"I mean that there is nothing more between Lady Olivia Dunbar and myself."

"And what has happened to cause this amazing turn of events?"

The baron smiled cynically. "My eyes have been opened to her true nature."

"What the devil do you mean?"

"I mean, sir, that the lady does not care one fig for me. She has feigned an interest in me . . ." Ramsay paused and looked at the professor. ". . . in order to win a wager."

"That is poppycock," said Burry, regarding his friend in some astonishment.

"Would that it were. No, it is true. You recall that I first met Lady Olivia in London? You remember how odd I thought it that she and the Roxburys were so eager to make my acquaintance? You see, they had a bet that Olivia could charm me into proposing matrimony. It seems they thought me a great challenge to her feminine wiles. It was a great joke to them."

"Well, I find it very hard to accept such a story. Lady Olivia Dunbar is not the sort of woman to do such a thing. Besides that, she is clearly in love with you."

"And you, sir, are clearly mistaken. We have both been bamboozled by the lady."

"Who told you this preposterous tale?" asked the professor.

"Malvern. He was here before dinner."

"I cannot believe you would give credence to anything that man would say. He is a scoundrel!"

"He is, but even scoundrels may tell the truth sometimes." The baron shook his head. "I went to see her. I had to know the truth. She admitted there was such a wager."

"Good God," said Burry, "but what else did she say?"

"That does not signify."

"But I should think it does. What did the lady say to explain herself?"

"She said she had given up the wager long ago and that she does love me."

"And you did not believe her?"

"I shall not be such a moonling again. No, Professor, I was very foolish to fall under her spell. I did think she cared for me. I even thought she had become interested in my work and was sincere in her praise of my book. How she must have been laughing at me."

"See here, my boy, I think you are mistaken."

Ramsay directed a warning look at the older man. "I pray you say nothing more about the matter, sir. Indeed, I never want to hear Lady Olivia's name spoken again."

"But Ramsay, I think you—"

"Please, sir, I must insist upon it," said Ramsay sharply. He rose from his chair. "Good night, sir. I wish to retire." The baron left the library followed by the dog.

Now alone in the library, Professor Burry shook his head and then stared glumly into the fire.

24

After spending a sleepless night, Olivia rose early. Restless, she decided to go riding. Putting on her sky-blue riding habit, she called to Mayflower. The little hound was ecstatic at the prospect of going out and eagerly followed her mistress from the rooms.

As it was still early, Sophie and Aubrey had not yet risen. Olivia announced her plans to the butler and went out to the stable, where she had a groom saddle the gray mare. She refused the servant's offer to accompany her and, after being assisted into the sidesaddle, tapped the horse's sleek flank with her riding crop and was off.

The air was brisk, but the morning sun shone brightly as Olivia made her way down the village road. Indeed, it was a fine day for riding, although Olivia was scarcely aware of it. She was very much preoccupied with thoughts of Ramsay.

After riding for a time, she came to a crossroads and purposely turned her horse in the direction opposite Hawkesmuir Castle. Knowing that Ramsay had no wish to see her, Olivia thought it would be very awkward meeting the baron. He thought she had made a fool of him, and Olivia knew that he would never forgive her for that.

She frowned and tried to think of other things, but she soon realized that it was useless to try to keep Ramsay from her thoughts. She continued her ride intent upon her gloomy reflections.

She heard the sound of the huntman's horn in the distance and, pulling her horse up, gazed across the countryside. The Malvern Hunt! The thought of the squire made Olivia's frown grow deeper. He was the most odious man she had ever known. She imagined him regaling his hunting companions with the story of Ramsay and the wager. Doubtless they would all have many laughs at the baron's expense.

Mayflower had pricked up her ears at the sound of the horn, but the sudden appearance of a rabbit was a much more enticing diversion. She dashed off in pursuit. Olivia smiled indulgently as the dog raced gracefully across the moor, and then she redirected her attention toward the sound of the hunt. She could hear the hounds and knew that they were on the scent.

The gray mare pawed the ground and seemed eager to join the hunt. Olivia held her firmly in check. "No, my girl, no hunting for you today."

Then, as Olivia continued to stare out into the open country before her, she caught sight of a fox. The creature ran swiftly, weaving across the moorland. To her surprise, the fox turned suddenly and headed directly toward her. Coming within fifty feet of Olivia, it stopped abruptly, a startled look on its face. Olivia and the fox stared at each other for a brief moment and then the animal bounded toward the almost impenetrable thicket known to the huntsmen as the Claxton Covert.

Olivia was relieved to see the fox dive into the covert and vanish from sight. In the brief glance she had exchanged with the creature, Olivia had experienced a strange empathy with the fox. She had sensed its fear and desire for escape and had wanted it to get away. She thought suddenly of Ramsay's abhorrence of hunting, and for the first time she could understand his feelings.

The barking hounds appeared, followed by the horsemen. Olivia saw Malvern leading the hunt and felt some satisfaction in knowing that the hounds would have much difficulty ferreting the fox out of the covert. The dogs howled with excitement and ran past Olivia into the thicket.

The squire, who was following the hounds, pulled his horse up beside Olivia's. Malvern nodded to her but seemed much more intent on the hunt. "Damn," he growled, watching the hounds move about the thick covert, "the Claxton Covert."

"What a pity," said Olivia sarcastically.

Malvern frowned at her. "You're not still vexed with me about yesterday?"

"I am more than vexed with you, sir. Not only did you behave abominably to me, but you showed yourself to be a scoundrel by going to Ramsay and telling him lies."

He grinned unpleasantly at her. "You should be grateful to me for ridding you of the fellow. He's not enough of a man for you, my girl."

Olivia glared at him. "Lord Ramsay is more a man than you will ever be, and he is a gentleman as well. You, sir, are an ignorant bully!"

The squire was surprised by the vehemence of Olivia's words, but before he could reply, they were joined by some other riders. Olivia, who did not wish to speak to anyone else, kicked her horse and rode quickly away. Mayflower, returning from her pursuit of the rabbit, and very excited at the sight of all the other dogs, nonetheless followed after her mistress.

Olivia had not gone very far when she realized that she wanted only to see Ramsay again. She must make him understand, she told herself. Thus resolved, she directed her mare toward Hawkesmuir Castle and urged the steed into a gallop.

It was not long before she arrived at the castle. Jem, the

servant who took her horse, seemed very glad to see her. "Good day to you, m'lady."

"Would you look after my dog, please?" asked Olivia.

"Very happy to, m'lady," replied the servant, who then watched with interest as Olivia went to the door and pounded the knocker with resolution.

The door opened and the butler greeted her. "Lady Olivia."

"Good morning, Hardy. I must see Lord Ramsay."

"I am sorry, my lady, but his lordship went riding. I do not know when he will return."

"I am very happy to wait, Hardy. I do not care how long I shall have to do so."

"As you wish, my lady," returned the servant, ushering Olivia inside and escorting her to the drawing room.

Once alone, Olivia paced across the room in some agitation. After a time Professor Burry entered the drawing room. "My dear Lady Olivia. I am so glad you have come."

"Professor Burry."

"Do sit down. I fear it may be some time before Ramsay returns."

Olivia nodded and then sat down on the sofa. The professor sat down across from her. "Perhaps you know why I have come," she said, regarding Burry with a serious expression.

"I know something of it," replied the professor. "Ramsay told me of your wager." Olivia looked down and Burry continued. "He is very upset. He is so much in love with you. The idea that you care nothing for him has broken his heart."

Olivia began her reply, completely unaware that at that moment Lord Ramsay had arrived at the doorway to the drawing room and had heard Burry's remark. "Oh, Professor Burry, I do care for him! You must believe me!"

"But what of this wager? Is it true that you pretended an interest in him?"

Olivia reddened and nodded reluctantly. "I know it was horrid of me. Yes, I do admit that at first it was a joke. I tried to charm Lord Ramsay as a lark, but very soon I called off the wager."

"You realized that you were wrong to have made such a wager?"

Olivia smiled. "No, sir, it was that I realized that his lordship was impervious to my charm. Indeed, we both disliked each other heartily. It was a blow to my vanity to find a gentleman who found me so easy to resist."

Burry smiled. "And you did not come to Northumberland to pursue the wager?"

She shook her head. "Of course not. I came here because I could no longer endure living in my brother's household. My sister-in-law was continually plaguing me about getting married. I could not bear it and so I came with the Roxburys to Fenwyck."

"Your sister-in-law plagued you about getting married?" asked Burry.

"She found it difficult to accept that I had completed my fourth Season in town without accepting an offer of marriage." Olivia smiled again at the professor. "I met many gentlemen in town, but until I got to know Lord Ramsay, I never wished to marry."

"And you wish to marry Ramsay?"

"With all my heart. I am so much in love with him. Oh, Professor, I think I began to love him when he found me on the moors that night. I had never met anyone like him. He is so different from the gentlemen I know in town, who care only for the cut of their coats and sport. Lord Ramsay is so kind and intelligent, and the most interesting man. I confess that I had always thought history a bore, but Lord Ramsay has made me see it very differently." She paused and regarded Burry earnestly. "Oh, Professor, I must convince Lord Ramsay that I do love him. You do not think it is hopeless?"

Professor Burry smiled sympathetically. "It is not hopeless, my dear, but I fear it may be difficult. Ramsay was so very hurt.''

''I know,'' said Olivia. ''Perhaps I can never expect him to forgive me.'' Tears began to roll down her face. ''If he rejects me, I do not know what I shall do. I shall never love anyone the way I love him.'' She buried her head in her hands and sobbed.

The professor looked dismayed and, glancing toward the doorway, caught sight of the baron. Ramsay motioned him to remain silent as he entered the room. Olivia was too distraught to notice his lordship's approach. The baron pulled a handkerchief from his pocket and handed it to her. ''Thank you, Professor,'' she sniffed. Glancing at the handkerchief, she recognized it as the one she had given Ramsay. She looked up and saw the baron. ''Gervas!''

''Ramsay,'' said Burry, ''Lady Olivia has come to speak to you.''

The baron gazed down at Olivia, who was regarding him entreatingly. ''I heard everything you said to the professor, Olivia.''

''Oh, Gervas, can you ever forgive me?'' she said.

The baron replied by snatching Olivia into his arms and enfolding her in a tight embrace. He kissed her hungrily again and again.

The professor, quite delighted, hastened away and shut the drawing-room doors behind him.

''Oh, Gervas,'' said Olivia rather breathlessly after the baron had finally taken his lips from hers, ''I love you so much.''

''And I adore you, my darling.''

She gazed up at him. ''I am so glad you have forgiven me.''

''You must forgive me for being such a muttonhead. Say you will marry me.''

''Yes, my dear Gervas. I want nothing more in the world than to be your wife.''

Thrilled at this reply, the baron pulled Olivia to him once again and kissed her passionately.

"Lady Olivia!" The sound of Geordie's voice brought Olivia and Ramsay back to reality. Disengaging from their embrace, they regarded the boy in some embarrassment. However, Geordie was not in the least abashed at finding his uncle kissing Olivia. He grinned. "Excuse me, uncle, but I saw Mayflower outside and knew Lady Olivia must be here. It was a surprise because I thought you would be out hunting with the Malvern."

Olivia smiled at the lad. "I do not think I shall do any more hunting, Geordie."

"But, Olivia," said the baron, "I would not prevent you from doing so if it is what you wish."

"But I do not wish to hunt." She looked at Geordie and smiled. "I saw a fox today and he and I came to an understanding about the matter. I am grateful to that fox because he made me think of your uncle and helped me decide to come here today." She glanced over at the baron. "And I am so very glad that I did come."

"So am I," said Geordie. He glanced expectantly from Olivia to Ramsay.

The baron smiled. "What would you think of my getting married, Geordie?"

"If you are to marry Lady Olivia, I should think it a very good idea indeed!" cried Geordie.

Olivia laughed and embraced the boy. "I'm so glad you approve, Geordie."

The boy grinned and kissed her on the cheek. "I'll wager this will be the best wedding ever!"

"My dear Geordie," said Ramsay, "I think it best if we have no wagers here for a good long time." He directed a stern glance at Olivia, who laughed again. Geordie regarded them both quizzically, but neither the baron nor Olivia provided an explanation. "Go and fetch Professor Burry," said the baron. "We must tell him our news."

Geordie nodded and raced off on his errand. As soon as

he was gone, Olivia smiled up at the baron. "I know I should say nothing more about the wager, but, in truth, I think I am the most fortunate woman to have won it."

His lordship smiled in return. "My darling Olivia, it is I who have won."

Olivia looked into Ramsay's eyes for a brief moment, and then, throwing her arms about his neck, she kissed her baron joyfully.

About the Author

MARGARET SUMMERVILLE grew up in the Chicago area and holds degrees in journalism and library science. Employed as a librarian, she is single and lives in Morris, Illinois, with her Welsh corgi, Morgan.

AMOROUS ESCAPADES

☐	THE UNRULY BRIDE by Vanessa Gray.	(134060—$2.50)
☐	THE DUKE'S MESSENGER by Vanessa Gray.	(138856—$2.50)
☐	THE DUTIFUL DAUGHTER by Vanessa Gray.	(090179—$1.75)
☐	THE RECKLESS GAMBLER by Vanessa Gray.	(137647—$2.50)
☐	THE ABANDONED BRIDE by Edith Layton.	(135652—$2.50)
☐	THE DISDAINFUL MARQUIS by Edith Layton.	(145879—$2.50)
☐	FALSE ANGEL by Edith Layton.	(138562—$2.50)
☐	THE INDIAN MAIDEN by Edith Layton.	(143019—$2.50)
☐	RED JACK'S DAUGHTER by Edith Layton.	(144880—$2.50)
☐	LADY OF SPIRIT by Edith Layton.	(145178—$2.50)
☐	THE NOBLE IMPOSTER by Mollie Ashton.	(129156—$2.25)
☐	LORD CALIBAN by Ellen Fitzgerald.	(134761—$2.50)
☐	A NOVEL ALLIANCE by Ellen Fitzgerald.	(132742—$2.50)
☐	THE IRISH HEIRESS by Ellen Fitzgerald.	(136594—$2.50)
☐	ROGUE'S BRIDE by Ellen Fitzgerald.	(140435—$2.50)

Prices slightly higher in Canada.

Buy them at your local bookstore or use this convenient coupon for ordering.

NEW AMERICAN LIBRARY,
P.O. Box 999, Bergenfield, New Jersey 07621

Please send me the books I have checked above. I am enclosing $_____
(please add $1.00 to this order to cover postage and handling). Send check
or money order—no cash or C.O.D.'s. Prices and numbers are subject to change
without notice.

Name_____

Address_____

City_____State_____ Zip Code_____
Allow 4-6 weeks for delivery.
This offer is subject to withdrawal without notice.